I0764568

WAIL!

AN AMERICAN JOURNEY

BORGO PRESS / WILDSIDE PRESS

www.wildsidepress.com

Cover design by Highpoint Type & Graphics
Barbara Biggs & Ethan Moe, Editorial Assistants

Library of Congress Cataloguing-in-Publication Data

Burgess, Brio, 1943-
Wail! An American Journey / by Brio Burgess; edited by Gail G. Tolley and Daryl F. Mallett
p. cm.
ISBN 1-877880-12-4. -- ISBN 1-877880-13-2 (pbk).

WAIL!

An American Journey

A Novel
in
autobiographical vignette form

by
Brio Burgess

Edited by Gail G. Tolley
and Daryl F. Mallett

advertised on
www. Daryl Mallett.com.

Published by Jacob's Ladder Books
A Division of Angel Enterprises

2002

WAIL!

An American Journey

Dedicated to Mary Jane Burgess

"Poor Mother, sometimes she'd whale hell out of us with anything she could lay her hands on."

William Carlos Williams from Autobiography of William Carlos Williams. New York: New Directions Paperback, 1967

Dedicated to James C. Burgess Sr.

"The front-line soldier I knew had lived for months like an animal, and was a veteran in the fierce world of death. Everything was abnormal and unstable in his life. He was filthy dirty, ate if and when, slept on hard ground without cover. His clothes were greasy and he lived in a constant haze of dust, pestered by flies and heat, moving constantly, deprived of all the things that once meant stability -- things such as walls, chairs, floors, windows, faucets, shelves, Coca-Colas, and the little matter of knowing that he would go to bed at night in the same place he had left in the morning. A front-line soldier has to fight everything all the time. It makes a difference in a man's character."

Pyle, Ernie. BRAVE MEN. New York: Grossett & Dunlap, 1943

Focus: An Introduction

The Twentieth Century awoke to war in its teens. Gradually becoming engulfed in a celebrated revolution, a country was born that didn't live up to its expectations. Untold millions died from influenza, assassination, destitution and relocation. After World War I, many young Americans embarked for Europe. Paris became a teeming community of bohemian aspirants. Writers, painters, poets, philosophers and sculptors appeared as practioners of the arts. They were in league with and courted by eccentric entrepreneurs from Oakland and San Francisco, California. During daily walks and promenades along the quays, money was spent on the works of obscure European painters and sculptors ...

In England, a Missourian via Harvard had a nervous breakdown brought on by the pressures of his job in a bank, his aspirations and his wife. Switzerland was Eliot's place of retreat. It was in a sanatorium there that he recovered enough to contact Pound about his new "long poem". Pound helped him create a handle he could sell. The Waste Land was born while an Irish novelist with an arrogant eye wrote the story of one day in the life of a couple of rowdy Catholics in Dublin. He called the epic Ulysses, which became known as the first novel of the 20th Century ...

Thereafter shadowy Eliotonian heroes wandered through literary Waste Lands of existence that lasted beyond the madness of the '20s, the sadness of the '30s, the horrors of the '40s, until the accusations of the '50s spawned another poem. Ginsberg's HOWL was heard around the world as a call to arms.

Howl ushered in a savage age of wolves characterized by packs of roaming youths clad in coats of colors. The colors, worn as suits of armor, identified family, territory, turf, crib ... colors were the coats of arms of these new knights of the open road. Cribs were castles, turf was kingdom. Youths wandered through worlds their fathers' experiences had forged for them. New rites of passage were characterized by the ability to survive the electric Kool-Aid Acid test of LSD and marijuana, with occasional cocktails of cocaine and heroin. How could outer space be explored before one had mastered inner space?

Mars was the agenda of the 21st century. That far-off planet of dry barren dusty red rocks seen through telescopes for centuries, Mars became the new frontier, as exploration of psychedelic consciousness had been the pioneering event of the 20th Century. By the 21st, the Bible was referred to by some as the "Book of Instructions Before Leaving Earth" ...

Earth had become a place of tragedy. The cities of the Blue Planet were filled with hordes of walking wounded. Scientists and politicians looked towards the red planet anxiously, in search of a place they hoped to one day cultivate as a refuge from Earth.

WAIL! AN AMERICAN JOURNEY by Brio Burgess

from the projects of California to a viable place in Eastern mainstream society, through the worlds of the streets, the arts and various forms of employment and other human experience, one person's perspective on life in the second half of the 20th century in our country...

PART ONE: "PUSHED BY THE WIND" 7-68

In which we meet most of the major influences in the author's life and visit various turning points from the perspectives of both yesterday and today.

In which we see the seeds of experience grow to fruition and observe the Soul's dark night as it makes its way to maturity, incorporating all, leaving nothing behind.

In which we encounter some of the products of this author's journey, and hear some last observations on the path her life has taken ... impressions and expressions ... concrete and abstract.

PART I

PUSHED BY THE WIND

PART ONE:

PUSHED BY THE WIND

Preface: Soup Line

The people waiting for the soup...
Some are so hungry they settle for lukewarm.
They are tall, short, fat, thin,
large-boned, frail, susceptible to illnesses.

Thinking people, they wonder "why".
Why are they so hungry, they are ill prepared
to die -- they stand in waiting silence...
I hear the people's cry -- "Help Me!"

The above poem describes the drawing on the cover of this volume. Both drawing and poem are the work of Mary Jane Burgess. Her life and her work at the Jesus Center Soup Kitchen/Mission in Chico, California and other places during the 1980s and 1990s inspired these creations. She is mentioned repeatedly throughout this book, dedicated to her in recognition of her survival and that of most of her children.

****

"San Francisco Summer:1968"

****

Riding along the freeway, looking out the window, wishing there was some way to wake up in the morning without having to get a shot ... wishing to be like the people who only had to have a cup of coffee to get them going.

The buildings of the city raced past as the car shot towards its destination, the same place we always went these days: the stucco house out in the Sunset, to park the car, to climb the steps, to go into the apartment where we spent most of the day every day. My old man was a "Mother". It was 1968 in the city; business was booming.

I'd only signed on for the summer. It was empirical research. I'd already discussed it with my New York friends at a dinner party in 1967 in Saratoga Springs, New York. I'd asked, "Is there a better way to find out about something other than doing it?" The conversation was philosophical, concerned with the accuracy of results gathered through experience rather than reading about things. The response was positive: one of my friends had answered, "When there was a war, and we wanted to know about war, we went to the war..."

There was indeed a war going on in 1967 in the U.S. and I was part of it. It was centered in my hometown, the one I'd run away from a couple of years before, the famous City by the Bay known for its Golden Gate and Acropolian topography, seven hills surrounding a fortress of gold. There was a saying, "The miners came in '49, the whores in '51; when they got together, they made the native son ... "

When the hippie movement hit in the Summer of Love, 1967, I was back east, drinking myself to death with brandy and burgundy. This cocktail, laced with old-fashioned wartime Benzedrine given to me by one of the local kids, was fueling the creation of thirteen mad paintings, one of my summer projects. I was doing them in acrylics and oils, in variations that I'd learned from a woman with whom I'd lived in Sausalito, in a broken wooden castle on a hill with a gigantic view of the city. In the morning when the fog rolled in, the spires of the skyscrapers floated above the clouds, giving them the appearance of being celestial ...

Jean Varda, an artist from France who'd been one of Picasso's students, lived on a barge on the waterfront of this hamlet, and painted celestial cities that looked like this skyscape of San Francisco, floating above the clouds of the early morning dawn. Alan Watts, the infamous Zen scholar, lived on a boat next door. They would often breakfast with each other, and in the early '60s my friend and I would go there as apprentices. I'd never seen men with such red faces! At the time I had no idea how famous they were, or why. Eventually I ascertained that their complexions came not from the sun, but from the wine they drank. There was always a gallon of burgundy on the table in the kitchen/living room of Varda's barge ...

I don't believe we had coffee for breakfast in those days either, but back then I was nineteen and on my own, with a friend named Barbara who said I could also have a job at Varda's, helping to make the birds for the walls of the Greek restaurant in North Beach that he'd been commissioned to decorate ...

****
"Cut to the Chase
****

The first, last and only time I was ever arrested was in 1956. I was thirteen and in a homemaking class at a high school on the Peninsula in San Mateo County, California. It was the spring semester and suddenly there was a note delivered to the teacher of the class. She came to where I was sitting and said, "Bria, you're to go to the principal's office."

I gathered up my books and notebook and trotted along the corridors, past the winding staircase that went up to my history class to the Administration office. A policeman was waiting for me there. When I was introduced to him he said, "Come with me."

Silently I followed him to the parking lot, where he opened the door of his car for me and told me to get in the back. It was the first time I'd ever ridden in a police car. There was a wire partition separating the front seat from the back, the same kind of screen some of the New York City taxis have today.

We swung down the hill that the high school was on and drove along El Camino Real, past my parents' house on Santa Maria Avenue, past the El Motel where I used to swim with my grammar school girlfriend Margie, past St. Dunstan's School where I'd fainted in the schoolyard from kidney disease and had to spend two weeks in the hospital when I was eleven. Finally we drove into the parking space in front of the San Bruno City Jail.

The policeman stopped the car, got out, opened the door for me and led me up the front steps. Inside the stationhouse, he handed me over to a uniformed matron who took me into another room and told me to take off all my clothes. The woman then ordered me to step into a shower stall where she physically inspected me, which was very embarrassing. Afterwards she turned on the water, adjusted the knobs that regulated the flow and temperature and asked me what I had done. I had no idea of what it could be, but in jest I replied, "I tried to rob a bank."

After the shower I was given a towel to dry off with, told to get dressed and then taken to a cell. Not the kind with bars, but one with a little glass window at the top of the door, and opaque glass on one wall. I was put in without my schoolbooks. There was only a cot and mattress, a sink, a toilet, a chair and across from the cot a big black glass that I thought must be a two-way mirror.

I sat for a while, stunned, looking around, looking up at the ceiling tiles full of holes and at the glass wall I couldn't see out of, and at the black mirror that I was sure was two-way. I counted the holes in the ceiling for a while, and then looked under the bed. There was a roll that someone had tossed under there. I got it and ate it, dry and stale as it was. Then I fell asleep.

When I woke up it was because of the door opening. One of the officers had brought in my brother Jimmy to be a prisoner with me. Jimmy was ten. He asked me why we were there. I told him I didn't know but that it must be something to do with mommy. Then the officer brought in my sister Mari-Beth. She didn't know any more than we did.

Then we heard the screams. I started to shake all over and feel frightened. I knew it must be Mother. I couldn't imagine what had happened but knew something had. She'd probably flipped again. She'd only been eating pan-fried potatoes lately, and hadn't been able to feed the new baby because her milk wasn't thick enough. She'd been calling up the social worker asking for another food order for the past couple of days, ever since Daddy had taken off, as he did from time to time after one of their fights.

It still haunts me, the screams, sounds a wild animal makes when cornered, when wounded, when her cubs have been taken from her, when she's been locked up in a cage. I was the only one in the cell that was tall enough to see out the window. I looked out and saw my mother, standing between cops and social workers, with her arms held back by a belt. Tears were streaming down her face; she kept saying the same thing over and over again:

> "Give me my children. Hail Mary, full
> of grace, the Lord is with thee...
> Holy Mary, mother of God, give me back
> my children... "

They just stood there, in front of the cell door, in the hallway of the San Bruno City Jail in 1956 on a late afternoon. Cops, social workers, and my screaming, praying, supplicating, begging mother. Her crime had been that she asked for one too many food orders. She'd gotten on one too many bureaucrats' nerves. So some social worker at the County Department of Social Services had told someone to get out the wagon and call the police department, that they were going to shut this woman up once and for all: how dare she keep asking for food orders?

They'd stormed the house. Another Waco, Texas before Waco, Texas; another Move in Philadelphia before the Move on the Movement in Philadelphia with helicopters and tear gas, and finally burning the house down. Well, this premonition of the "war against the poor" happened in San Bruno, California in 1956 on Santa Maria Avenue in the neighborhood called Lomita Park.

The kids that were home with my mother on that afternoon were armed as ninjas from the Japanese fields. When the police and social worker came to take them away to the orphanage, Mother ordered the children to charge the agents of control with sticks, brooms, hoses, chairs ... there was quite a ruckus. The accompanying social worker picked up the baby that was lying in a crib on the first floor. Telepathically my mother knew what had happened, and she charged down the ladder to the door. That's when they nailed her. With a leather strap around her arms in lieu of chains, she was shackled to a policeman and led away to the patrol car.

She had led the children in the "standoff" as though once again she were leading an army of warriors, as she had in the play, "The Warrior's Husband" so many years ago, when she'd performed in front of 2,000 spectators at the Cow Palace when I was in her belly. She was an

Amazon; she was the warrior waiting for the return of the Argonauts. That was in 1942-43, and here she was playing the part again, only this time instead of Greek tragedy it was American Black Comedy, commedia del arte, if someone ever staged it, someone like you or me, or the ghost of Genet or Cocteau.

Someone could make quite a play out of this scene. It was the scandal of the county at the time, until almost everyone there who remembered it either died or went on to other things. And what did the poor woman get for her valiant attempt to keep a family fed?

She got a sentence to Agnew State Mental Hospital, with the prescription of electroshock therapy, untilshe forgot the facts of her life that had allowed her to act like that over a food order, of all things. She was there for a few months, diagnosed as paranoid schizophrenic, a catchall phrase in the psychiatric community, as AIDS is in the medical establishment.

I think that her insanity was from malnutrition. She'd suffered from it for years, at least thirteen years. Now the medical profession is just beginning to realize and teach that various forms of psychosis originate with malnutrition ... a polite word for starvation!

Starvation: a state of chemical imbalance, of under-nourishment. I starved myself for years, off and on, to find out what it did to people. To find out what it had done to my mother, that she should act out in such a fashion, and be punished so brutally for crimes she never intended to commit.

None of the things my mother did were premeditated.

They were all spontaneous reactions to the life-threatening situations in which she and her children were constantly finding themselves.

****

"Albany Notes: August 1995"

****

First thing, first day of the workweek, the boss is using his insidious control techniques, telling me to Xerox this and "do it now" ... but then it is a Monday morning ... Tony Bennett is singing "I Left My Heart in San Francisco" on WABY 94.5 AM radio, the home of "The Greatest Melodies of All Time". Office work can be deadly to one's spirit, but there are worse things ...

Over the weekend I read almost all of the new book USER by Bruce Benderson about the life of the male hustlers in Manhattan. Puerto Rican, black and Irish queens, transvestites, crack heads, speed freaks, junkies ... with names like Angel, Tina, Baby Pop, Angelita ... the setting reminds me of North Beach in '64, although it's nothing like it, except that the story narrates the activity of a small circle of acquaintances. They're the people who don't wake up till 1 a.m. because that's when it's safe to score on the streetcorners of Times Square.

I've ordered The United Nations of Times Square from the Stuyvesant Plaza Book House, same author. User is his third book; the first one can no longer be found in Books In Print.

Ladies are now sitting on the client bench, speaking Spanish, as a little girl comes out of the Day Care

Unit with a toy she'd found there. A social worker is Xeroxing work on the copier. The office is busy for a Monday morning at the end of August. I'm drinking tea at my desk -- don't drink coffee any more -- and take Ginsana for my breathing. There's an item in the newspaper today that Timothy Leary has cancer of the prostate, and that he's dying. The report of his enthusiastic acceptance of this condition is a tremor of the temper of the times.

Also of note: 2.7% of the adult population in the U.S. is in prison or on parole. Page A-3 of the Monday 8/28/95 Times-Union further states that "since 1980, the number of people in prison or jail or on probation or parole has almost tripled, growing at an average rate of 7.6% a year."

I've also been busy this morning ... "Where they coming from?", one of the workers remarks on his way out to get some water for his tea. "The streets", the secretary replies, shaking her head for emphasis ... why would one need to ask?

****

"Musings: Sausalito 1963"

****

As the moon sailed through the sky over the city of skyscrapers rising in silhouette across the bay, I was running around the outside of the houseboat on Gate 5 Road. It was 1963. Marsha and I had just moved there from San Mateo, runaways, able to pay the first month's rent but not knowing how we were going to pay on the month to follow.

Our landlord Tom Considine, a tall, skinny,

beautiful guy, owned a lot of houseboats. This was the legendary neighborhood of Jean Varda, Alan Watts and Ale Eckstrum, besides countless other beatniks, bohemians, Korean War vets and runaways. Gate 5 Road wasn't the most spectacular neighborhood. It was full of mud in the rainy season ... but there was a certain magic about it, an ethereal, otherworldly quality that colored everything beautiful. The same feeling was in the Tides Book Store, the Kettle Delicatessen on Bridgeway, the Sandal Shop run by Anne and Ollie, and Juanita's Galley. The foghorns in the morning, the seagulls as they flew over the mud flats, over the piers ... it was so elegant, like some third world country.

Living on a houseboat in Sausalito in 1963 was like living on a junk in China. The boats were so close together, and everybody knew each other. Juanita's Galley, also called the Charles Van Damne, was the biggest ferryboat there. It was a 24-hour restaurant/after-hours joint/nightclub, with red checkered tablecloths, tabletop jukeboxes and seats by the windows looking out on the mud flats, where the seagulls strolled so gracefully, just like a scene from somewhere in India, or perhaps Taiwan.

Of course it could be recreated. All we'd need is a gigantic ferryboat with everything intact, a streamlined Juanita's, with 24 hour a day coffee and donuts, soup, hamburgers, cokes and jukeboxes. No liquor! There would be vets in charge of the work shifts ... that's how it was. I guess that nowadays we couldn't find the same kind of help. Today we'd hire the homeless, those who had it together, that is, and a family would soon form itself as it did before.

How much waterfront land would be needed? How much would it cost? Who owns it today? The Whole Earth Magazine people are on Gate 5 Road now ... the seagulls, foghorns and mud flats are still there too, along with the skyline of the city, and the view of the islands and the bridges ... the original Never Never Land ... though now the cliffs of Sausalito are studded with decks and studios, precariously clinging to the side of the mountain, and the old unfinished Hearst Castle has been turned into condominiums, rising up above the Bridgeway skyline.

In those day there were 42 bars in a space less than three miles long in Sausalito. We used to go from one to the other just to see who was there ... from the No Name to the Two Turtles, the Bridgeway Inn, the Seven Seas and the Glad Hand, which had been the original Tin Angel, on up to the Trident, then the Valhalla, which was the capstone experience.

The Valhalla, notorious nightclub of famous ex-San Francisco madam Sally Stanford, author of the book "Lady of the House", once the mayor of Sausalito ... poor little rich girl! Jack London had been a frequent habitué of the building that became the Valhalla. He'd been a rumrunner! So many times Juanita used to tell me the stories that were still spoken of, the legends surrounding the building that became Sally's restaurant ... they used to row the stuff ashore, liquor from Oakland in those days, silently, in the dead of a moonless night, when only the lapping of the waves could be heard. They'd dock the boat under the building and then go inside for drink. In that time the building was an inn, with a trap door that opened to the underside where the boat was moored, and that's how they got the liquor up to the shelves from which it was subsequently served.

I remember one afternoon, perhaps in June of 1963, Juanita and I were driving around Nob Hill in her black station wagon, en route to Sally's residence on Pine Street. We were going there to help Sally dust her cabinets, because she wanted her things to look nice for the ghostwriter of her book, "Lady of the House". Also, I don't think Sally wanted to be there by herself the first time she met him. So, there I was, dressed like an elf with black tights, purple and black tunic and white blouse, lace collar and lace cuffs. When Sally objected to the wearing of my black elf shoes on her white rug, I took them off and walked around in my stockinged feet and did as I was told.

Eventually Juanita said that she had to get back to Sausalito and that I could ride back later with Sally. That was the first time I'd ever been in a Rolls Royce. I was terrified. To me, Sally Stanford looked like she had seen absolutely everything evil that man could conceive of or do. To my eyes, at that time, her life was written on her face.

Many months later, Juanita got me a job at the Valhalla as a hatcheck girl. One of my duties was to help Sally on with her shawl every night. When I did this I was shaking inside, but I didn't want her to know it. Now, as I look back on that scene from the distance of time, I realize that I must have been suffering even then from some kind of chemical deficiency. After all, why should I have had such stage fright about helping an old lady on with her shawl every evening unless I was in some stage of chemical imbalance?

Many years later, they finally made a movie of "Lady of the House", and I watched it on TV in Albany, New York with my companion Gail, and told her that I'd met the person that the story was about, that she'd been the oldest of a large family, and had been poor and gotten a bad deal ...

Meanwhile, it is after midnight here in 1996 in Albany, and Gail just called to say that she'd be home shortly. She's been working overtime, to put it mildly. The dogs are all collapsed in the living room on their couches and chair: Tip the Labrador, Wrinkles the foxhound and Pippy the Beagle. I cleaned the cats' room earlier and fed the residents therein. There are four cats living in the basement to keep away the rats and mice: Blackie, Tigger, Grey and The Big. Each one has a separate story, as do each of the dogs. Well, there'll be another day at the office tomorrow, and so I'll say goodnight.

"Poverty: 1950s California"

The paupers' dole in the America of the 1950s did not have all the fringe benefits of the 1990s. There were no food stamps, no school lunch programs, no WIC, no feeding or other form of maintenance program for poor pregnant women. There were housing projects and food orders.

There were commodities such as the mystery meat that

had been chicken once, until all the taste had been boiled away and only chalky gobs of overboiled flesh remained in jars with equally overcooked noodles. There were also cans of what we called dog food, some sort of cold beef, also without taste. The containers it came in were big, like 2-pound coffee cans. Families in need would go to the government warehouse to pick up the items on certain days, as they still do today.

In 1953 in South San Francisco I remember seeing these items, along with sacks of corn meal, regular flour and powdered nonfat dry milk that always looked blue after it was made up. There was also rice and macaroni shell pasta. I remember eating a lot of Spanish rice, made with tomato sauce, onions, green pepper and little bits of cooked hamburger scattered through it. I remember macaroni with never enough -- or without any -- cheese. Macaroni shells with salt, pepper and margarine for dinner, with blue milk on the side and corn bread into which Mother had cooked bits of onions. Exciting diet, wasn't it?

We'd supplement it with green mint tea, made with leaves that grew along the side of the house. I'd go out and pick some, come in and boil water to pour over the leaves. After the tea had steeped, I'd add Karo syrup, as there was very little sugar, and Karo syrup was one of the commodities on hand.

There was an old lady who lived across the way from us with her husband in the housing project. She would bake the biggest sugar cookies I ever saw, and put them out on her window still to cool. Every Saturday morning, we'd go across the street to her yard where the swing set was, and we'd swing and pretend that we weren't waiting for her to call us to come and get a cookie.

After that we'd go down to the railroad tracks where there was a hobo jungle. Bushes full of blackberries were there, and we would take empty coffee cans with us, fill them up with blackberries and carry them home. We'd wash them, and then make a dough of flour, water, baking powder and salt, roll out the dough and put a bunch of berries mixed with precious sugar in the middle. The sides of the dough would be folded up like an envelope, and this would be put into the oven and become a blackberry cobbler. I also remember rhubarb pie and sweet potato pie. Once in a while my mother would bake these items for a special treat.

When she was pregnant, my mother would have a craving for pigs' feet. She was pregnant a lot. They didn't have vitamin tablets in those days the way they do today. If a woman developed a nutritional deficiency when pregnant, she just had to live with it ... and so did her children. My mother had many, many pregnancies, and never fully recovered from one before she'd begin another. The malnutrition kept growing bigger and bigger, as did her aberrant behavior, until it all culminated in a massive blowout as described earlier. Charges of multiple felonies result from assaulting police officers, and so they threw the book at her.

She recently told me that she used to get horrible three-day headaches. I've had such headaches in my life, and recently my sister Mari-Beth over the phone asked me if I still got them. I told her no because of the medication I've been taking. She told me that she still got headaches, and that a doctor had told her he wouldn't give her any medication because of her genetics. I asked my doctor about this and she said that there were many different medical theories and left it at that.

My medication is a serotonin reuptake inhibitor (sri) similar to Prozac, I've been told. It relieves depression and anxiety with undesirable side effects, varying with the individual, from weight gain to weight loss and loss of libido. They didn't have such medication in the 1950s. My mother had 36 electro-shock treatments instead. After that the headaches went away. Of course she'd still flip out but not in the same fashion as before, although I do still remember beatings on Peninsula Avenue in San Mateo in 1961, years after her treatments had supposedly broken the cycle.

"Albany Journal Notes: Winter 1996"

January 2: Just got back from walking to the Price Chopper Supermarket and back in the latest mini-blizzard. It was tiring toward the end. Felt a cold spot on the top left side of my head, so blew into the scarf around my face, directing the heat up to the cold spot ... it worked. Then I was comfortable, walking along, carefully stepping in the safe areas with no ice. I unpack the groceries, hopefully enough for the next few days, and go upstairs to write another page of prose.

Earlier was reading a scene from Charlie Chaplin's autobiography. He'd played British music halls and American vaudeville shows for quite some time before getting the "big break" that got him into the film business ... and then even when it came, the offer to work with the Karno company, he didn't recognize it for what it was, but quite arrogantly asked for more money ...

February 14: Valentine's Day. First thing this morning my pup Wrinkles butted me in the face as I lay in bed to get up for first play with him ... left a small red mark on my upper lip ... and I have a horrible cough, dry when I run out of cough syrup, that lingers on. It's the cold! Minus 25 degrees wind chill yesterday. It's going to be in the 20s today, but with cold winds from Canada.

March 1 is my five year anniversary date with the County of Albany, New York and I'll have three weeks of new vacation time to spend, and better weather to spend it in.

My sister Mari-Beth called, saying that Mother had gone on a bus to Sylvia's in Texas and was telling her that she (Sylvia)was crazy, and that she (my mother) was going to take her children away from her. And Sylvia was so upset by this that she'd called Mari-Beth as to what to do, and she was going to call the police to have Mother taken away.

I called Sylvia up and suggested that she should buy Mother a house in Texas so she would have her own business to take care of and not want to interfere with Sylvia's, that she should get Mother a house next to an oil field, so she could get involved with looking for oil ... black gold ... and then the thought got into Sylvia's head and she clicked onto it that yes, she could buy Mother a house on a piece of property for $30,000.00 and then Mother could have a thrift store there and sell Brio's books, Mari-Beth's clothes, Veronica's paintings, Sylvia's whatever, her own hats.

Sylvia told me that she had a 1990 Jaguar and I told her I wanted a 1935 Model A Ford someday, and she told me that she had four 18-wheelers and trailers to go with them, and that our brother Philip was a good mechanic, and I told her about my book "Street Kids" and how it could be a movie and asked if she would back it, and she said maybe, after she'd gotten through with all the other stuff she's involved in.

****

"North Beach, San Francisco, 1961"

****

We finally found a parking space. After driving around the streets of North Beach for what seemed like hours, although it was really only a few minutes, anxiously looking out the window, excitedly saying,

"There's one ... "

"No, no, we won't fit in there ... "

"Hey, look over there, he's pulling out ... "

"Yeah, cross your fingers ... "

"Just in time ... It's almost 9 o'clock ... "

"People are just starting to come out. It's early."

Parking the car, we scrambled out of it, taking to the streets as rapidly as possible. We were going to the Fox and Hound to see the proprietor, David Nelson. He had classically chiseled features, and was about six feet tall, with light brown hair and beautiful eyes. The Fox and Hound was a non-alcoholic folk music club on Upper Grant Avenue, down from the Coffee Gallery, but up from the Hot Dog Palace and across the street from the Capri.

We would go up to San Francisco every night if we had the chance because of the things that were happening there, especially in North Beach. There was a current of excitement in the air, an energy that wasn't present on the Peninsula. We were college kids in our late teens and early twenties at the time. We'd grown up in the shadow of a political climate that sparked a literary movement that gave rise to a civil rights era never before seen in the history of the world. We were on the move. We could feel that there were more things happening in the streets and cafes of North Beach than were happening in the schools and homes that we so happily ran from to the midnight crowd in the city ...

****
"Sausalito 1971: The Tin Angel"
****

Other pictures flash before my mind's eye. Early mornings waking up on a long plush orange couch to look out a set of square paned windows at a view of the whole San Francisco skyline. For ten years I thought of someone else's house in Sausalito as my home. It was a safe house, a place I used to go to cry, and to hide out. A place I used to go so I could clean up for my friend who was crashed out, resting after her devastating life. My friend Peggy, who was the first one to put jazz on the San Francisco Embarcadero. Her nightclub, the Tin Angel, was across the highway from Pier 16, written about by William Saroyan in his play, The Time of Your Life. Peggy was an entrepreneur from the old school of nightclub era gangster days.

She was also an artist, and in the 1950s had the longest-running show in the history of the De Young Museum at the time. Her paintings were toys, objects that people wanted to touch, done with thick frosked paint put on with a spatula in the style of Van Gogh and Rousseau. Copies of some of them adorned the record covers of the white jazz artists Paul Desmond and Vince Guaraldi, whose tunes "Take Five" and "Cast Your Fate to the Wind" enhanced the San Francisco Sound of the 1950s Renaissance. It was the time of Lenny Bruce's nightclub act and Allen Ginsberg's "HOWL".

I remember once upon a time in Sausalito as though it were yesterday, walking up the hill from Bridgeway to Cooper Lane, to the wooden castle on the hill that was a refuge for myself and my brother Tony for ten years.

****

"Albany Musings: March 11, 1992"

****

The desk at which I write at work has a wall beside it, of gray material studded with posters of performances. Performances of music and words, of poetry and play readings, of past events and happenings. In the daytime I work as a clerk in a Social Services agency and sometimes play piano at night in a local nightclub. We pass the hat for donations after the evening of neon blues and psychedelic cues. Sometimes we have more of an audience than we expected. Dave plays electric and acoustic bass, Michele plays tambourine and later uses it to collect donations from the audience for our troupe. Occasionally Doc sits in on alto sax. I play acoustic and electric keyboards and jazz flute. Angel plays drums and Gail intersperses the introductions and intermissions with folk songs from the 1960s, '70s and '80s ... occasional originals round out the program.

We change our names frequently. Sometimes we're the Neon Blues, sometimes the Homeless Haiku, and other times we just call ourselves Street Kids. We've been in Albany, New York since 1981 and have been performing together since the 1981 Pinksterfest, when I played backup on electric guitar with Gail on an open-air stage in Washington Park. Our sound was carried out over the miles of lawn by loudspeakers. This was on a summer Sunday, shortly after we'd arrived in the Great Northeast from the sunny slopes of San Francisco.

San Francisco, of course I miss you! The walks along the Great Highway, through the streets and alleyways of Chinatown and North Beach. The dismal rooms in the haunted cheap hotels. The dealers fighting in the upstairs corridors and hallways. The crash of bodies slamming against walls, into doors, knife blades flashing against a background cacophony of hideous screams. The feeling of uncontrollable violence that permeated the walls that seeped inside the rooms in which terrified residents waited for a body to come crashing through the door, into the room that was referred to as home.

And so it was in San Francisco in 1980 that, one

night at 4 a.m., during one such dealers' fight, there was a knock on our hotel room door. My mother had suddenly, spontaneously decided to come to San Francisco to see how I was living. She was loaded with hundreds of dollars she'd won in a suit against the State of California's Social Services Department. Apparently a state car had bumped into the back of her car and given her a whiplash, causing her to wear a brace around her neck for months. The litigations had gone on for years and then, when she was finally awarded a paltry sum of money, the first thing she did was come to the city to visit her eldest child. Have mother, will run away! We spent $1,700.00 that day.

One thousand dollars was payment to a Chinatown realtor for a studio apartment on Nob Hill. It was a block up from Polk Street, where there were bars and jukeboxes that blared songs out into the night. These were the sidewalks where teenage runaways sold their bodies for dinner or a place to stay, always open to relationships that might rehabilitate them someday.

Just before I left San Francisco I was horribly sick for two weeks with a deadly pneumonia in the apartment that we'd rented on that day. I had to stay home from work. I couldn't talk. My throat was raw; it hurt to swallow. It was impossible to cough up the deadly pea green phlegm with spots of red scattered through it without hurting, as convulsive tremors shook my body. I had to write to friends for loans to get medicines of lemons, honey, Vitamin C and Vitamin E, B complex and multiple vitamins. One of the women at my office said that the Presidio had sprayed the city with a virus they were experimenting with to use one day in germ warfare. She said that the army would then check the emergency rooms of the local hospitals after the spraying to see how many cases of this rare and virulent pneumonia had showed up for treatment. I was inclined to believe her at the time, and wondered if that virus had anything to do with the pneumonia usually reported in cases of AIDS.

I finally recovered enough of my health and voice to return to work after exhausting my sick leave and vacation time. Shortly after this terrible pneumonia, I resigned from my permanent job and relocated three thousand miles away, to a small city in upstate New York.

Albany, New York, the oldest still-operating city in North America today. Dear Albany, a sweet little city cradled in the Valley of the Gun, on the path to empire, surrounded by the Adirondack Mountains and the Catskills. I've been in Albany since 1981 and do believe I've fallen under the same spell that Rip Van Winkle encountered that caused him to sleep for 100 years. Eventually, I should wake up with a Doctorate in Sociology, and then be able to help all those darling abused substance abusers, poor bruised flowers that they/we are. I can count several among my friends, my brothers and sisters and acquaintances, not to mention my own youthful experiments with disorientation of the senses, and those of others I have come to know: Arthur Rimbaud, Vincent Van Gogh, Amodeo Modigliani, Charles Baudelaire, Edgar Allen Poe, Charlie Parker, Billie Holiday, Steve Comacho, William Burroughs, Neal Cassady, Ken Kesey, Jack Kerouac, Allen Ginsberg ...

****

"Steve Comacho"

****

Steve Comacho, the guitarist who took me to Sausalito that first time, so long ago ... I saw him again in 1973, on a drizzly San Francisco night as I was coming through the Stockton Tunnel. There was a fellow walking ahead of me, a tall man in a long dark raincoat and a hat, and as I passed him on the narrow sidewalk, I recognized his face. It hadn't changed in eleven years. He hadn't changed in eleven years.

I said, "Don't you play the guitar?" He stopped, turned to look at me, and said, "Yeah". I said, "Didn't you play 'The Sun Rises' song from 'Black Orpheus' for me at Coit Tower, a long time ago, and then you took us to Juanita's in Sausalito for Sunday breakfast, and we read the comics, and you had two dancers with you? I was with a kid named Jonathan."

As he looked at me, his eyes lit up in recognition and I said, "What're you doing now?" He said, "I've gotta go to a pharmacy to get some Quaaludes for my old lady. Hey, where you live? Maybe I'll drop by some-time." I said, "I got a room at a hostel on Post Street, the Post Street Residence Club, on the third floor near the phone ... yeah, stop by ... " "Okay," he said as he hurried off into the drizzly mist of another San Francisco night.

I watched him disappear into the shadows, wondering if I'd ever see him again, realizing how extraordinary it was to have run into him again at all after all those years. But then San Francisco's a small town, especially if one was born in it, as I was.

But when Steve did get around to visiting me I wasn't able to open the door to him, and I've felt terrible about this ever since. How could I tell him that I was afraid we'd both be busted if I let him use my bathroom, that I was "hot" because of the plays that I'd been putting on in San Francisco in 1973, and because of the dangerous lifestyle that I'd adopted?

How could I tell him I'd had tracks on my arms for nine months in 1968 because of the things I'd been doing with my old man -- no, I couldn't tell him that I thought the room was bugged by the military guys that lived across the hall, or perhaps by the fellows with the tape recorder who had brought all this reel to reel equipment to my room to tape some of my songs, and had been able to talk to each other through what seemed like some kind of intercom. They were all too close for me to be able to feel safe with Steve. Dear Steve, if your tired old junkie ghost is looking over my shoulder as I write this, I hope you finally forgive me for not opening the door to you that night so you could use the bathroom.

Hey, I've met an old friend of yours back here, Angel Cupril. He was in the movie "Ironweed" with me and Jack Nicholson and Meryl Streep and Tom Waits and Lena Spenser and so many others ... "Ironweed": that was the movie about down-and-out alcoholics in Albany, New York during the Great Depression. The story's set in 1937 ... alcoholics going down slow ... the hallucinatory scenes were, I think, the best part of the show. The first shot in it is of the body of Jack Nicholson wrapped in cardboard and newspapers, sheltered by a wall in Troy, the city next door. The camouflage is so effective that it's impossible to tell that there is a body inside the debris until it moves. Angel and I both played derelicts in the movie, and talked about you. He was the one who'd told me that you'd died.

Hey, Steve, you know what happened after that breakfast we had? Eventually I got it together and moved to Sausalito. We rented a houseboat on Gate 5 Road with money my boyfriend had borrowed from his mother. I had to get away from San Mateo County! Juanita had moved from her bait shop restaurant where we'd eaten that morning to the Charles Van Damme sitting on the water on Gate 5 Road. I worked there for tips as a waitress and table clearer, sometimes a stove cleaner, until the place was closed down by the Feds. There was a rumble there one night between the Marin City Spades and the Hell's Angels. Juanita's written a book about it and so now it's all history! But in 1963 it was a haven for me.

Then I left the State of California one day in 1965 in a blue Sunbeam. We drove across the country, two weeks on the open road in a blue sports car. Terrible things happened to us during that trip ... I almost got sold into slavery, Steve, and almost got killed. But we managed to escape and make it on through, stopping at truck stops and thruway restaurants until we got into Amsterdam, New York. I laid low at the driver's grandparents' house, and worked as a waitress in a bowling alley for a while until the heat blew itself away.

To get away from Amsterdam one night, I'd asked

my friends to please take me away from the land of the Headless Horseman to a place where artists and musicians play. I'd written a play there, in the hours after working at the bowling alley, called "Sausalito Fairy Tale". It was only one act, and the pages were covered with candle wax because that's the only light we had in that empty room off the living quarters of Kimberly's grandparents.

It was a play about the things that Peggy used to say ... the dialogues we used to have in front of the fireplace in that broken wooden castle on the hill, the home we lived in. That house in Sausalito was my home for ten years, off and on. Ten years! I would run away, and be brought back, and then I'd run away again, and then be haunted by Peggy ... telepathically haunted until she died in 1973 in the Marin General Hospital, of cancer of the colon and diabetes. Sometimes she haunts me still.

But Steve, I think of you also, and feel bad that I was so paranoid that night, so mad ... as in crazy ... but I was afraid that if you came in and pulled out your works to fix that we would be busted and that is why I sent you away so coldly. I hope that you can find it in your heart to understand. Junkie saint, one of my many brothers on this planet, may you rest in peace today ...

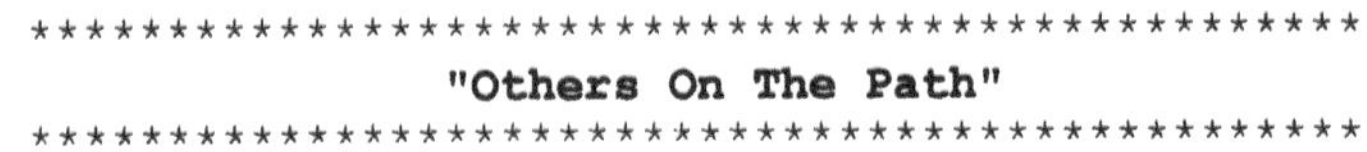

"Others On The Path"

Along the road, a few of the poets I've met, and others that I've read: In 1964, in a bar on Upper

Grant Avenue, Michael McClure asked me if I could tell him where to score the speedballs people were doing, and I had to tell him no! Then I saw him again in 1974. I was going out the door of the ACT offices of the Geary Theater and he was going in. I was a temporary typist there and he was the playwright in residence that year.

In 1986, the ashes of the poet Bob Kaufman flew into the sky. Some say he drank himself to death in a bar on Broadway in North Beach. After winning a literary award from the National Endowment for the Arts, he was able to buy drinks every day. It was $12,000.00 all at once: more money than he'd ever had at any time in his life. I read that in a press release put out by Lawrence Ferlinghetti, who bankrolled his funeral, a jazzy affair with a 12-piece band that paraded through the streets playing the "St. James' Infirmary Blues".

I used to meet Bob Kaufman in the rain in San Francisco, while walking through the streets of that old town from Market Street to Chinatown. It was a daily thing. The last time I saw him was in 1980 in the Swiss American Hotel in North Beach, at the end of the block on Broadway, just before the thruway to the Berkeley bridge. We were there at the same time, just doing the usual things.

His funeral was big, going all through the streets of Oakland as thousands of people met to follow the procession. They tossed his ashes into the San Francisco Bay from a boat, Jacques Micheline, Lawrence Ferlinghetti and other members of his family. A friend of mine in San Francisco said that it was a blonde that did him in, but only Bob knows if it was the blonde or the alcohol.

Perhaps it was just the stress of success after so many years of obscurity, so many years of police brutality and general indifference. He came from a family of 14 children, born of black and German-Jewish parents in New Orleans.

Neal Cassady died on a railroad track in Mexico in 1969. He was stoned and out of his mind, spending his last few moments stumbling down the steel highway looking for the next long ride. His life would make a great movie. His autobiography describes a poor kid growing up on skid row in Colorado with his father and the other rambling men that hung out together then. The book, called The First Third, was published in paperback by City Lights and then reissued with endorsements and a preface, testifying to the life once lived by another poor little down and out Chaplinesque kid.

Jack Kerouac died of alcoholism at his mother's home in Florida a number of years ago. There was a dedication in a park in Lowell, Massachusetts a few years back. Some of his words had been chiseled into blocks of granite to commemorate the life he'd written of when he was far away. All his old friends and enemies showed up to read the words in memory of this literary sage who gave all that he had for the story on the page: his mind, his body, and finally his life.

Jacques Micheline, one of Kerouac's old friends, lived in the San Francisco Bay Area, and liked to wander through the streets of the cities, wherever he found himself. Sometimes billed as a New York Street Poet, he'd been around for a long time. I first met him in 1973, and then again in 1980 I bumped into him on Sixth Street in San Francisco. He wanted to go for coffee, but I was in too much of a hurry going from pawnshop to hotel and back again on an errand for a friend, so didn't have time to stop to chat and have a cup of cheer. I'd gotten a few letters from him since coming back east. He said he liked my jazz pieces ... and then the letters stopped, because I'm in another lifetime now than the one I used to know while wandering the streets of San Francisco ...

In the New York Times today I saw a clipping about a new opera. Allen Ginsberg and Peter Glass have collaborated on a piece they called "The Hydrogen Juke-box", playing full-blast in May 1991 in Brooklyn. When Ginsberg read in Albany in November of 1990, six hundred people went to hear him at the event, sponsored by the Writers's Institute. He was amazed that so many people were there, so many people who wanted to hear the voice of a poet who's been censored for so many years. I gave him the clipping about his reading in the local paper, so that he might have a memory of Albany, New York and of the audience he has there ... a memory for a scrapbook of publicity to look through some day, when he's more old and gray ...

****

"On the Road: 1977"

****

The highway was cast in light of orange neon night as the rain poured down. Cars speeding past splashed through lakes appearing in the contours of the freeway.

The woman hitchhiking along the side of the underpass was cold, drenched, shaking from her flight. The rain was washing away all the pain.

A car suddenly slowed down, moved to the inside lane and pulled up just ahead of the woman. She walked toward the door, looked in. The driver, an elderly man, old enough to be somebody's grandfather, rolled down the window of the limousine.

"Where you going?"

"Sacramento. Then I can get a bus to San Francisco ... "

"I'll take you a ways down the road. Get in."

"Thanks..."

As the hitchhiker got in the car, the driver adjusted his gearshift and pulled away from the curb, speeding off into the night.

Soon the warmth of the inside of the vehicle began to penetrate the frozen skin of the passenger. It was a silent ride as pictures of the past few hours flashed through her mind. She had to steel herself to face the tragic reality of her mother's insanity. She'd been trapped by knowledge of the brutal futility of life with her genetic family for as long as she could remember.

As the car sped along the highway, the woman turned back into a girl, running from a town she'd never lived in, a life she'd never asked for, along a road she didn't want to travel. It was a road on which she found herself because she knew no other way to make it through each day, one day at a time.

****
"Flash Back: The 1950s in California"
****

Remembering the poverty of those old days when we had commodities on our kitchen shelves and neighbors with numbers from concentration camps on their arms doubles the apprehension I feel when reading that one B-1 bomber costs two billion dollars. There's so much money for weapons that we don't need, and hardly any money for women and children. How much could one do with two billion dollars to help eliminate illiteracy and unemployment in America! To the Pentagon, billions of dollars is nothing. When talking about the price of weapons there is no limit. But when addressing the needs of poor women and their children, everything is expensive.

I remember the Christmases we used to have with my family. There would be food baskets from the Church and the county. My grandparents would deliver nicely wrapped store-bought presents. The packages looked inviting from the outside, but the contents were always the same boring necessity items: usually school clothes for the boys, sturdy shoes, flannel long-sleeved shirts,corduroy pants. I don't remember getting any presents from my grandparents that could be considered fun.

My father would make toys for us: carved trucks, a chess set, and there was a large piece of furniture that looked like a church pew from the chapel of a castle. It had a seat where we put the music books that went with the piano that he sometimes played. My father was an artist. He drew thousands of character sketches on pieces of white typing paper. My mother would scream at him for hours for drawing these figures when he should have been thinking of ways to make money.

****

"Flash Forward: San Francisco 1973"

****

... remembering those rainy San Francisco nights ... wandering into North Beach after making the rounds ... the Sheraton Palace cocktail lounge, the Saint Francis cocktail lounge. After work I'd go in past the Fu dogs that guarded the entrance to Grant Avenue ... sometimes I'd just pass these sculptures, hurrying on to the Stockton Tunnel, where the latest street legends were illustrated as 20th Century pictographs on the walls of this tiled porcelined gallery. Graffiti on the walls told prices and descriptions of the medicine of the underground: China white, Mexican brown, Acapulco gold, Tai stick, opium ...

****

"Flash Back: Alameda County, California 1948"

****

We were living in a housing project in Richmond. I'd gone with a girlfriend to her house. It was a stucco building next door to mine, a three or four floor walkup, only her apartment was on the ground floor.

When we got to her house she opened her refrigerator and took out a big jar of white stuff that I had never seen before. Then she got a couple of pieces of bread and put the white stuff on each piece. She gave me one and took a bite out of hers. I took a bite out of mine and tasted something gooey and sweet. I had never tasted anything like it before. I asked her what was on the bread and she said, "Miracle Whip". I said, "What's that?" and she said, "Mayonnaise". I had never heard of mayonnaise before.

A short time later, I got sick and had to go to the hospital. I remember that when my mother brought me home from the hospital there was a dead cat on the doormat in front of the entrance to our apartment. I was alive; the cat was dead. The image of that instance haunts me still. I was four years old, not in school yet, and had had scarlet fever. They'd treated it at St. Mary's Hospital in San Francisco, and hadn't given me penicillin for it. The disease had permanently damaged my kidneys: glomular nephritis.

What a way to go! with a disease that only shows if you eat animal protein ... be a vegetarian or be on dialysis. Can you imagine what it's like to have to be on a dialysis machine, eight hours a day for a couple of days a week to replace your blood, all because of food?

****

"The Artist's Colony"

****

In 1969 I was awarded a fellowship to Edward MacDowell Colony in Peterborough, New Hampshire. It was called the Edward Arlington Robinson Fellowship and it covered the cost of my four-month stay in the Addams and Starr studios, named after Jane Addams and her partner, Ms. Starr, who initiated the institution of compassionate social work into American society. Their work with immigrants and others at Hull House in Chicago, Illinois during the 1920s and '30s spawned what is today known as the U.S. Department of Health and Human Services.

James Baldwin's name was among those appearing on the wooden plaques on the mantelpiece of the Starr studio. He was a guest at MacDowell Colony during the forties and fifties before he went to Paris. He came from the streets of Harlem, growing up in poverty, surrounded by despair and the insanity that often springs from it. He grew up wild.

I came across a description of him written by someone who had known him during the 1940s when he was still a young man. He was once described as coming out of the night, looking like a junkie trying to score. Of course he was not a junkie; he was only keeping an appointment he'd made with a colleague he'd met in a bar. But he was unable to shake the reflection of the environment he existed in on a daily basis. He looked and acted like the world that he came from: the savage world of poverty. A world where malnutrition and insanity walk hand in hand, as they oft times spring from each other, and are as closely relate as mother and daughter, father and son. The medical establishment has yet to publicly acknowledge this with the same degree of enthusiasm that is reserved for other findings, yet it needs to be stated if society is to improve.

****

"1993: Where Are We Now?"

****

Albany is such a small town, but it's said to be the drug capital of the Upstate New York area. Apparently a lot of cocaine traffic comes through here. Also a lot of infamous outlaws, such as Legs Diamond, Dutch Schultz, Meyer Lansky and Joe Adonis made money in Albany, New York in the '20s and '30s. Across the river is Troy, once the location of daring underground railroad rescues during and before the Civil War of the 19th Century. Up to the north is Saratoga Springs. One of my friends from there in 1967, Dr. Grace Swanner, wrote a book called Saratoga: Queen of the Spas, an analysis of the mineral springs of the area. They have great bottled water back here. There is also quite a bit of seltzer water, which we drink a lot of in Albany.

The Price Chopper Supermarket is the most popular 24-hour nightclub in the city. It is owned by the Golub family, who also own a chain of bookstores, and sponsor the holiday fireworks displays here. Going to the store is an extravagant luxury for people who spend most of their time in offices providing services to the community and in schools upgrading their skills. After all, there are only 24 hours in a day, and so much to be done within that time.

There are so many colleges in this area that I finally decided to avail myself of one after being back here for ten years. Since the fall of 1990 I've been attending Russell Sage College Evening Division, earning a B.A. in Sociology. I have 87 credits and a B average thus far. There's nothing else for me to do in Albany, just work and go to school.

During this time of my life I feel as though I was in some kind of suspended animation. Working as a clerk-typist for a county agency from nine to five

Monday through Friday is not the most stimulating way to make a living ... but it beats the streets any way you look at it. Just get there on time every morning, answer the phones, get the appropriate person when someone comes in to apply for day care or protection or some other service.

There are so many people requiring services today ... millions of casualties of the 20th Century. What are we going to do in the future, when there aren't enough hands to fill the needs of the people?

Once I get my Bachelor's, I'll go for my Master's and then a Doctorate in Sociology. It's a new discipline, only as old as the 20th Century. Maybe someday I'll be able to make a movie from my books, with all their characters from my past. I still remember the days before food stamps and Pampers ... the days before Medicare and Medicaid ... the days before Albany, New York, and my East Coast excursion.

****

"Memories: the LSD Experience"

****

The first time I had acid was at the Carousel Ballroom one night in 1968. As I was traversing the staircase with the crew I'd just dropped with, we approached the gigantic full length mirror above the entrance. I saw a twiggy shorthaired girl in a short blue trench coat, gray dress with lace at the cuffs and collar and blue high-heeled shoes. I instantly thought, "Lois Lane, Girl Reporter" while running up the stairs to the balcony.

From above, as I looked down at the crowd below, I

saw my old man with his white Panama hat circulating through the dancers. As I glanced at the band gyrating on the stage, in the distance the wall across the arena exploded in patterns of kaleidoscopic colors, as though the universe was being created all over again, and Earth was being formed again, and once again God was being the best Artist of us all.

The planets' history unfolding before my stoned eyes were the pictures I saw that evening. Earth's rhythms appeared to be vibrating through concentric circles of exploding time. These were the psychedelic impressions coming from my mind ... catalyzed by ergot ... crystallized in mime ...

It was a forbidden underworld, that land through which I used to wander, but I didn't know it then ... I didn't think that way. I was with my childhood friends. People I'd gone to junior college with. I'd known them all for such a long time ...

A couple of years later, I heard the cuckoo's lullaby ... and voluntarily sought out this sound, for which I'd cried. It's the song of a broken hearted frail lost in a long, haunting wail ... the anguish of a mother who's had her children taken from her ... I think that's the reason behind the cuckoo's cry ... also behind the Irish Banshee's sigh ...

****

"Thirteen Days in 1970"

****

The ward holds 80 women, forty beds on either side of a partition. Twenty beds along each wall, near the windows, and another twenty beds divided up along the partition across the room. Each patient has a bed, and next to each bed there is a night stand. The patients have no property other than their purses and suitcases, if they came into the hospital with such things.

Meds are distributed each morning, promptly at 6:30, and then breakfast is at 6:45, a big meal of porridge or cold cereal, toast, coffee and juice, and then the patients are left to "nod out" on their medication until lunchtime. Some of the women on the ward are recovering alcoholics; others have been committed by their families. One woman told me, while we were playing Scrabble, that her husband checked her in periodically when he grew tired of her, and then he would come and get her out in six months when he wanted the house cleaned thoroughly.

There wasn't much to do on the ward, other than wait for the seven cigarettes that the State authorized the nurses to distribute at 7 p.m. every evening, a humanitarian concession to the consumer-oriented addiction. Almost everyone on the ward smoked. We'd settle for butts and stubs after the cigarettes were gone. When I wanted to get out I volunteered to mop the ward floors and the bathrooms. Other patients on the ward were too stoned from the meds to be able to think of such simple activity.

I was locked up for a total of thirteen days, having volunteered for the assignment. I'd never been in such a place before, and there isn't much written about such places that conveys the actual nightmare existence of them. Of course this ward was supposedly better than the "Snake Pit" of the movie made to depict the scandalous reality of the asylums of the world.

While I was there I typed, after mopping the ward. I typed a thirteen-day journal describing the other inhabitants and myself. The story, called "The Orange Nightmare", conveyed descriptions of the stark existence of life on the miscellaneous ward of a New England state mental hospital in the 1970s.

****

"Sausalito: The Tin Angel Continued"

****

She always used to say, "You're going to miss me when I'm gone ... ", and she was right. The world hasn't been the same without her. Peggy was a person of the "old school", a folk musicologist who made me learn to read the notes to the songs that she liked to sing when she was"in her cups", quite often around 4 a.m. These drug- and alcohol-inspired performances always got her into trouble for making so much noise at such a delicate hour of the day.

Peggy got my brother Tony a job at the Kettle, a 24-hour delicatessen in Sausalito owned and operated by Leo Kerkorien, one of her old friends from Black Mountain College days. This job was great for Peggy, Tony and me. We didn't have to worry about food anymore with Tony living at Cooper Lane. Peggy rented him the spare room in exchange for sandwiches from the Kettle. This was in 1969, shortly before I took off on a jet plane for Saratoga and a fellowship to the artists' colony in New Hampshire.

I'd made a deal with Peggy to redecorate her house on Cooper Lane in exchange for rent. Tony supplied the food I ate, usually brown rice and sardines, and I'd roll cigarettes from a pack of Tip Top tobacco atop a pink-streaked round marble table top with a real Tiffany lamp hanging from the ceiling above it. There were also eight other lamps, full-moon globes, hanging in the living room of this haven/sanctuary. One evening I decided to put different colored bulbs in each one of the globes. From the lane leading up to the house, the effect was as though there were eight different colored planets hanging in the space above our living room ... orange, purple, blue, green, red, white, yellow and violet. I entertained myself with this light show for awhile, until Peggy said to change the light bulbs back again because the image of the hanging planets was "too startling" from the lane.

Peggy had a car, a Model A painted pink and orange like a checkerboard, parked in the carport. It just sat there day after day, year after year. She hardly ever drove it; she said it needed a part or something. It was like a big toy, with the mechanisms for negotiating it all in plain view. The stick shift, the clutch, the brake, the throttle (usually called the gas pedal) were all either on the floor or coming up from the floor, and larger than they are in the standard shift cars of today.

This particular Model A was a convertible with a rumble seat. The once-new leather seats had seen much wear and tear; the vehicle was more like an Army jeep to me than any of the other cars I've ever known. One night I drove it from one end of Sausalito to the other. I'd come into town from San Francisco and noticed it parked outside the Valhalla, and no one was around. I got in it and drove, with my heart in my throat, around the curve that could have spilled me into the water, along the Bridgeway, past the stone seal that sat in the water on a rock as though it were real. I drove through downtown and stopped it across from the No Name bar. I had to call Peggy to come out and park it. She'd just left it at the other end of town and then gone off with someone, forgetting about it completely.

Peggy was frequently in the bars for the conversation and the drinks. Her club, the Tin Angel, was gone, sold to Kid Ory for a song. There had been another joint on Vallejo Street that she'd tried to operate by herself, but it was much smaller. The original Tin Angel was a big warehouse on the San Francisco Embarcadero in 1955 and 1956. It had been featured in a story in Life Magazine in the August 1956 issue, and also on the cover of a book of photographs called I Am A Lover, which had pictures of the Beats of North Beach between its covers.

Peggy herself was on the cover of the first Lenny Bruce album, called something like "The Interview", published by Fantasy Record Company. Listed as The Lenny Bruce Originals Vol. I, on the cover there's a photograph of Max Weiss, one of the brothers who owned the company at that time. Mr. Weiss is sitting at a table holding a gun, with Peggy's business partner Irmine sitting across from him. Peggy is sitting on the floor reading from her book called Pigs Ate My Roses. This was one of the covers of that album. There were several different photos of this trio in a variety of poses taken and put on different issues of that particular first Lenny Bruce record.

Peggy's picture of two dancing elephants appears on

Fantasy album 3234 titled The Paul Desmond Quartet featuring Don Elliot. On the back of this album there's a photo of Peggy and a quote by Saul Zaentz, now president of Fantasy: "The album represents the first serious attempt to fuse primitive art with modern jazz. The painting from which the cover was reproduced is a prime example of the art of Peggy Tolk-Watkins, who has long been the leader of the San Francisco Bay Area's primitive art school. Tolk-Watkins has a permanent exhibition on display at one of the nation's finest galleries, The Fallen Angel in San Francisco."

The rest of the words on the back of this illustrious album are by Mort Sahl. These words and albums appeared on the San Francisco scene during the 1950s, the beginning of the Beat era. I've been able to find a few in the record stores and Fantasy Records catalogue. I gave one of these albums to Ferlinghetti in 1973 or '74. I didn't have a record player and was moving at the time and knew that City Lights would be a good home for such an item. These albums are part of the Beat Jazz history of the San Francisco '50s scene.

In 1971 when I became pregnant because of an indiscretion and was considering having the baby, Peggy asked me to illustrate a new edition of Pigs Ate My Roses. At that time, while hanging out in bed trying to carry the baby, I drew a picture of each poem for her and mailed them to her. She had 100 copies of it printed and didn't even give me one. I don't even know if she credited these drawings to my name. She was still angry with me for having left the house at Cooper Lane.

Shortly after the trauma of pregnancy, I went to work as a civil servant for the primary clerical agency in the country. It was a job and everyone needs a job. We all know that. This was in January of 1972. I moved to San Francisco's Weller Hotel, a single residency establishment in the Tenderloin neighborhood in back of the San Francisco Federal Building on Golden Gate Avenue. The hotel was a few blocks up from KGO-TV, the Bank of America and the Federal Building.

A Hindu family that filled the halls with the aroma of their curries were the landlords. They had beautiful brown thin children. The wife was only a child herself, and dressed in her sari every day. I didn't notice any signs of Americanization in their lifestyle or appearance other than the fact that they were American entrepreneurs. They were operating the hotel.

When I was at Cooper Lane I used to pick wildflowers all over the hills of the "Banana Belt" in Sausalito. That's what the curving road winding round the lanes and ridges of the Sausalito Hills was called. It was one of the wealthiest areas on earth because of its property values. Cooper Lane was a redecorated tennis club. It was rumored that the famous cartoonist Charles Schultz had once lived there, and had built the tree house on the property as a playhouse for one of his children.

At night the rafters of Cooper Lane would creak, as the wood appeared to be stretching. This would create all sorts of strange noises. When there alone, I could easily exhaust myself going up and down the stairs to the front door or out the back door to the garden to check for the cause of the noises. It might be skunks or raccoons going through the garbage or possibly a human intruder. The back porch was broken so that nobody could sneak up the stairs that way and break in. When we heard a noise or a knocking on the door, we'd look out the kitchen window which opened right over the lane and gave a perfect view of anyone that might be trying to approach. After I stopped living there and would go back to visit, I'd call up to the window and Peggy would stick her head out ever so cautiously, and then when she'd recognized me she'd say, "Oh, hi honey, I'll be right down ... "

Writing this is recalling events of over twenty years ago. Peggy died in 1973 at Marin General Hospital in Mill Valley. She'd contracted diabetes and then cancer of the colon, which had culminated in a disastrous operation. Peggy died shortly after I did my first show at the Mostly Flowers Gallery on Geary Street in San Francisco. She had encouraged my music, writing and painting. The parents that hadn't had time for me came together in Peggy. She was my parent for ten years. Her death pushed me into an abyss of oblivion from which it took me decades to extricate myself.

"San Francisco: 1973"

1973 was the year of my first production in San Francisco. It was a play called "Sir, Real Is Blue", at the Mostly Flowers Gallery on Geary Street. It ran on April 1, 15 and 30 in conjunction with the New York Post Card Show.

The set for the play was in the window of the gallery, which was illuminated by a blue light from twilight till dawn. There was a life-sized mannequin of a girl, dressed in the light blue nightgown. The mannequin was in a baby crib, with her finger pointed at the porcelain head of a matronly woman who represented her mother. Outside the crib, scattered about as toys the girl had been playing with. were aspects of the various American revolutionary fronts heard around the world during the 1960s. There was a headdress for the Indians, maraccas for the Chicanos, bongos for the Beats, and toys for the children, among other things. Some of the musics, presented through tapes that played during the show, were made with the kalimba, an African thumb piano. Part of the dialogue of "Sir, Real Is Blue" was a conversation among Gertrude Stein, Pablo Picasso, Igor Stravinsky and Alice B. Toklas.

The opening routine was set in a bedroom, where a boy and girl who had just made love were involved in discussing the intimate aspects of their relationship. The girl wanted to play her guitar and the boy didn't want her to. It was a situation about the girl's basic human rights, as opposed to the physical and psychological domination of the boy who was her lover at the time. On the three days of the full performance, the words and music of these pieces would drift out over the heads of the audience as they wandered in off the street from 11 a.m. till 8 p.m. The still life in the window remained on display night and day for the entire month of April, 1973.

During that time one of the officers of from the San

Francisco Museum of Modern Art came to see the exhibit. He told me that he thought the people of the Mission District wouldn't understand it, and I told him that I thought he underestimated the people of the Mission District.

As far as I was concerned it was a success, and after that piece of work I was asked to do another at the Intersection in North Beach. This second piece was called "Celebration", and was a workshop rather than a taped play. We prepared a live performance, but the management would not let it be performed live, "because it was a workshop". They turned the audience away at the door. After that I tried unsuccessfully to commit suicide and then went to live at Project Artaud.

****

"Albany Musings: 1981"

****

My partner Gail saved my life. There was a bullet with my name on it in San Francisco in 1980, because I was still alive and living the blues ... I first came to Albany in January of 1981, as a refugee from the streets of San Francisco.

I'd had an apartment in back of Nob Hill above Polk Street. My mother had rented it for me with her settlement money. I also had a permanent civil service job with the newly formed U.S. Department of Education. I was learning about the application of Civil Rights in elementary and secondary school situations while living with a turbulent soul, a darkly sinister filmmaker and expressionistic oil painter whom I'd known from the early 1970s San Francisco. We'd had a lot of acid together, exchanging minds and worlds. She was related to Edward Macdowell, who taught the first History of Music class at Columbia University in New York City.

Edward MacDowell was actually the first recognized American composer, who because of lack of adequate recognition here had gone to Europe to play his piano compositions. He returned to America with syphilis, eventually dying of it at his farm in Peterborough, New Hampshire. His wife was so distraught that she decided to turn the farm over to the Muses. She created an artists' colony out of it so that other souls like her late husband could have a place to work without having to undergo the humiliation suffered by artists who emerge before their time.

My colleague, Edward MacDowell's distant cousin, was crazy ... we were all crazy ... but I worked! When it got too crazy for me to work and continue to live in San Francisco, Gail took me 3,000 miles away to Albany and I've been there ever since.

****

"Lena's: Saratoga Caffe Society"

****

I wrote my first play in an empty apartment by candlelight in Amsterdam, New York in 1965. I called it "Sausalito Fairy Tale". The original script was covered with the drippings of the candle I had to use as light while typing the words late at night. Shortly after it was finished, we went to Caffe Lena, the country's oldest continuing coffeehouse, located on Phila Street in Saratoga Springs.

I got a job there with the Gallery Theater, which

was part of the coffeehouse. They put me in charge of the costumes, and then made me an actor in "The Corn Is Green", where I played a ten-year-old coal miner in corduroy pants with black dust on my face. John Wynn Evans, the theater director, cast me in this role. I was surprised when he suggested that I could play the part, never having thought of myself as being able to play a boy before I did it. It turned out to be fun. I hadn't read Germinal by Emile Zola yet, a book about 19th Century French coal miners. One of the miners is a 15 year old girl, Christina. It's a great read!

After that show Lena Spenser, the Caffe owner, cast me as Estelle in Sartre's "No Exit". We did it on the stage of, I think, a Methodist church in Burnt Hills, New York in the winter of 1966. Lena was paid $100.00 for the show, a lot of money in those days. During the imaginary waltz scene I forgot my lines, so I made some up on the spot and the audience didn't appear to notice, because at the end we got a standing ovation. The church was packed.

Lena had also gotten me a job dancing in a nightclub somewhere in Saratoga. I'd be picked up in a car and driven to the club, where I danced on the side of the stage in a cage, like a go go dancer, in black net tights and some kind of top. I don't remember very much about this other than going there, dancing, and then coming back to the Caffe. I don't remember getting paid; I guess I was part of some kind of deal that Lena had made with the club, where she got my wages in exchange for my room and board. I'd been involved in a similar deal in California in 1963 until I left ... what I'm talking about is a form of slavery, or indentured servitude, but because I was beholden to the people who got my wages, I couldn't get too indignant about it, and preferred to be amused.

Lena died of a heart attack in 1989, the winter of that year. She was on her way to Albany from Saratoga to attend a performance of Spalding Gray's monologue at the Egg. I was going to meet her there, along with some other people, but she never made it. Instead she fell down a flight of stairs at the Caffe on her way over. After that experience she went into a coma from the fall and never woke up. Lena was almost sixty-seven years old, and I don't think she'd ever paid the necessary social security taxes on herself ... she had been in the Caffe business since 1961.

After her passage over to the other side, a group of music lovers purchased the contents and the name "The Caffe Lena" for $2,000. This was the amount needed to clear Lena's name with the bill collectors. Eventually this new group, The Caffe Lena Foundation, was in need of $250,000.00 to purchase the building that the Caffe is in. Apparently the landlord wanted to sell it, and the price quoted was $300,000.00. At the time of this writing, the non-profit company that owns the name and paraphernalia of the Caffe Lena has raised the money. They have a website on the internet, follow the path of folk music ... Caffe Lena ... and it will appear, eventually ... caffelena@aol.com ... perhaps ...

When I met Lena one wintry night in 1965, she was acting the part of a Duchess in a play by John Ford. Spalding Gray was part of the resident Theater Company, along with Roger Robinson, John Wynn Evans and about 20 other actors and actresses from several acting schools in New York City. Spalding has gone on to achieve fame in various other areas, and has helped John Wynn Evans into a nursing home in Southern California. I've been told his daughter visits him. Roger Robinson went on to Chicago. I saw a photo of him with Lillian Gish once, awhile back.

While I was in residence at the Caffe during this early period, I kept journals containing stories, both true and fictional. In those journals I referred to these Gallery Players as "The Olympians", because that's how we felt at the time, while living together in a big Victorian house on Phila Street directly up from the Caffe, in the direction of The Grand Union Hotel and Broadway. The house isn't there any longer. The space is now inhabited by a restaurant and a parking lot.

I don't get to Saratoga that often any more, even though I live in Albany. Only a distance of thirty miles, if that, but without a car it's impossible to just "pop in and pop out". One can't just take a bus into Saratoga for a show at the Caffe or the Saratoga Performing Arts Center and hope to return the same day. One has to stay overnight! We used to sleep on the floor of the Caffe, or stay at Lena's house when she had one. Then we just stopped going.

The last time we were there when Lena was alive was in February of 1988 for a reading of one of my scripts, a four-act **musical play called included** in Street Kids and Other Plays called "Rooftops", aka "Broadway Blues". Lena read one of the parts, and called it a black comedy. After the reading, I played the score for her on the piano while Gail and Nick, the other two members of that Sunday afternoon Valentine's Day Company, went out to buy supplies for the Caffe from the local Price Chopper supermarket. Lena took a nap in the back room until their return. The lullabies I played helped her doze off ...

This is the same small company which had begun doing shows in 1987 at the Half Moon Cafe in Albany, after a music and words presentation at the State University of New York Performing Arts Center. That show was under the sponsorship of American University Composers, of which I was a member. All members had been invited to submit proposals for performances they'd like to do. My proposal was to do a show of original music and words illustrated with life-sized posters I'd made of my father's drawings of San Francisco street people. When I was notified that it had been accepted, I was thrilled.

During the 1970s my music played in San Francisco, Chico and San Mateo, California, and Saratoga Springs and Ballston Spa New York. In 1981 I opened the piano lid at the Lotus Club on 5th Avenue in New York City at the annual Edward MacDowell Colony Party and plucked the harp strings. From 1979-1984, Rod Summers of Maastricht, Netherlands published selections of my original music on piano and piano-harp with words on various cassettes both alone and with other artists. Selections from these cassettes were played in various countries around the world.

****

"San Francisco: Potrero Hill 1971/1973"

****

Project Artaud, now a successful Performing Arts Center in San Francisco, was created from a recycled American Can Factory that took up a number of blocks in the Potrero Hill District of San Francisco. Several hippie artists had been able to talk the city fathers and mothers into letting them have the building as an Art Center Cooperative. Artists would rent spaces and would call these places their studios. There were cooperative washers and dryers in the back part of the ground floor and on each level there were combination shower/bathrooms with lines of sinks and stalls. The inside reminded me of a high school, with its wide staircases and long hallways.

The first time I'd ever been to this structure had been in 1971, when I'd walked out there from North Beach to catch a poetry reading by a Russian who was quite popular at the time. I was acclimated to the night, but not to the darkness of that desolate street scene. As I was looking for the entrance, a red Volkswagen pulled up and three men got out, I later recognized them as Allan Ginsberg, Lawrence Ferlinghetti and Shig of City Lights Books. As I looked at them from the shadows I realized that they were the producers of the show.

A sign announced that the fee for the event was four dollars. I hadn't known that it wasn't free, and only had two dollars with me. I approached the trio and asked if I could have a pass, explaining that I'd walked all the way out there and hadn't known it was going to cost money. One of them handed me a pass and I hurried in so as not to miss the reading.

It was packed. People were wall to wall. Such

events staged by these fellows were always packed. After the reading, which also consisted of films, I walked back to where I was staying. I'd noticed that the air around Project Artaud was cleaner than that of the inner city. There wasn't much traffic out there then.

Almost three years later, after doing my show "Sir, Real Is Blue" in San Francisco and a workshop at the Intersection Church Theater during the spring and summer of 1973, I was living at Project Artaud. Some people who worked at the Intersection had arranged that I share a space in one of the studios. My "landlady" space-mate was Rosemary Eberhart, the spokeswoman for Project Artaud when anything had to be negotiated with the city. Rosemary was tall and lean, with long blonde hair, very ethereal looking, and reminded me of a muse from Olympus sent to help the hippies continue to "get it on" or recover from their bad trips. She'd put a life-sized poster of Billie Holliday above my sleeping bag platform to help me through. I was there "kicking" my bad habits, going cold turkey. It was horrible.

I was there for a month, most of the time visiting Eric Ryder, an instrument-maker who lived at Project Two, the smaller warehouse factory across the street. His space was full of automobile parts, musical instruments and the piano wire he used to string the inventions he made from other valuable junk he'd scavenged from the sidewalks and vacant lots of Potrero Hill. Eric later went to San Francisco State and became a physicist, but at that time music was the thing, and Eric was crazed the way he went about it.

He made fantastic instruments out of piano wire for strings and, in the case of his Cosmological Harp, the jawbone of a whale. This harp was played through the use of solar energy. The rays of the sun would bounce off a mirror, landing on the strings in such a way that sounds, similar to the tones of a whale, would emerge into the air. The Cosmological Harp was exhibited in various places, including the Palace of Fine Arts and at the World's Fair of that decade.

****

"Artaud Aftermath: 'Space Visions'"

****

Eventually I left Project Artaud and went to live on Sanchez Street in the Mission District, existing on unemployment, playing music and borrowing money to live on. I registered with an employment agency and went out to temporary clerical jobs. During this period the San Francisco Opera House called about the score that I'd delivered there earlier in the form of four audio cassettes that held the words and music to <u>Space Visions</u> aka <u>Chanson A Dieu</u>, played and sung by the author/composer.

One afternoon, the director's secretary called and asked for the piano-vocal score that went with the tapes I'd submitted. I had to look up what a piano-vocal score was, and then I had to make one. I did this in a week, writing while on my knees in the sansun position, putting the words and music into a coherent form. At that time I was supposed to be working on the opera with someone from the San Francisco Institute of Music and Art.

Our relationship terminated when he asked me to play the score on the piano. I felt embarrassed that I'd composed it on a nylon stringed classical guitar. I couldn't play the piano in any conventional way at the time. I'd created the music using the guitar and the kalimba, an African thumb-piano. Painstakingly, while on my knees for eight hours a day during those five days between jobs, I transcribed the score by first recreating the music from the tapes, then writing the notes down under the words after playing them together. I must have been enchanted, as it was an exacting exercise in precision.

Documentation concerning submission of this opera -- the fruits of all these labors -- can be found in a book in the library of the San Francisco Opera House, including the year it was submitted, its title, and the name of the author/composer (Brio Burgess 1974). I was 31 years old. Soon after that I left San Francisco for Saratoga Springs, New York on a Greyhound bus in the middle of the night, with a tape recorder and a shoulder bag ...

I'd had to leave five guitars in a closet on Prospect Street in the Mission. One of the guitars had been lent to me by Rodney Albin, Peter Albin's brother. It was an original handmade guitar. Another one had been lent to me by Roma Barons, whom I'd met in Saratoga in 1966 when she was playing there with Penny Lang and Rosalie Sorrels. I couldn't take them with me, and I hadn't been able to return them.

Eventually the words of Space Visions were published as one of the four plays that comprise Street Kids and Other Plays, with limited distribution in the United

States. "The Writer's Song" from the original opera was later published as part of a cassette of international selections by the British poet Rod Sommers in Holland in 1979, on the V.E.C. audiotape, "Still". As part of that collection, it was heard in 21 countries around the world, including over radio stations in Sweden and Australia. Rod also told me that it had even been heard on a rock and roll station in New Jersey!

At this time, Rod Sommers still lives in Maastricht, Holland and continues to publish, compose and perform, as do I and probably most of the other V.E.C. artists. His wife works with the displaced persons still wandering the Continent. World War disrupts lives for generations. Fortunes are lost, homes destroyed, documents eliminated, backgrounds forgotten, names desecrated and families broken apart forever.

One day when I asked Rod how Holland handled its homeless problem, he told me that his wife is one of the workers that cater to their needs. I found that tone revealing as to the difference between the cultures of Holland and America. Our young country has a lot to learn.

****

"Working In Albany: 1990s"

****

The front of the office is a plain glass door in one of the many small cities of upstate New York. It's an unobtrusive building on the corner of a block. The glass door is on a back side street, across from a parking lot and an overpriced restaurant. One wouldn't know what the building was, if one didn't know. The building that houses the offices has the name of a bank stenciled on the glass of the windows in the front. There is also the name of an upstate New York county across the granite above the front doors of the building. It had once been an Academy, and then it had been a Burroughs Business Machine Company. Since the late 1970s, it's been occupied by county offices.

Wednesday morning in June, 1993 ... there's a breeze blowing through the leaves of the trees. Various types of people are making their way along the sidewalks and highways, on their way to school, to work, to appointments. I'm one of those anonymous sidewalk commuters. I like to walk to work in the morning, rain or shine, winter, spring, summer or fall. This exercise replaces the tai chi that some people do in the early morning, preparing their bodies for the stress and strain of living.

But this story is not to be about me. This story is about a circumstance of life in which millions of people in America find themselves every day, all across the country. This condition of existence: poverty.

Most of the people on Earth in 1993 live in poverty. Hard to believe, but it's true. We know about the starving millions of Africa, India and Asia. We send food packages to the starving peoples of the fallen Soviet empire, and of the war-torn regions of Croatia. We contribute to the food pantries of our churches, communities and other charitable organizations. We give money in payroll deductions to the United Way, and sometimes we put change in the tin cup of the

Salvation Army soldier. We now see him on the street corners in early summer. I always remembered the Salvation Army from the wintertime, standing in front of the supermarket. Times must be rough these days, with these soldiers on the street corner on the oldest city in America even in the summertime.

I hear the streets of San Francisco are packed with poor homeless souls. It's easy to live in Northern California all year round with a couple of sets of similar clothes, such as jeans, tee shirts and tennis shoes. The weather is fairly consistent, with the occasional monsoon-type downpour. This kind of pounding, driving rain that drenches one to the bone, that no umbrella is able to withstand, this hard rain falls only occasionally in upstate New York. I've been caught in it on both sides of the country. The force of these storms so impressed me that I included their significance in a song. The piece goes like this:

"Been washed by the rain on the road,
kissed by the sun on the road,
pushed by the wind down the road,
been on the road so long,
the road's so long.

Everybody's on the road today,
don't make no difference what we do or say,
all gonna be pushed by the wind,
washed by the rain,
kissed by the sun anyway.

Everybody on the road today ...
Everybody on the road ...

PART II

KISSED BY THE SUN

End Part One

****
****

PART TWO:

KISSED BY THE SUN

"Preface: Neon Nights"

There's a Gulag on the streets
of the U.S.A.
late at night, at bus stops,
hanging out in 24-hour supermarkets,
cafes and coffee-carts,
in the all night restaurants ...

The Gulag of America's
on the streets of the U.S.A.
in the shelters and
the doorways of emporiums
today ...

crashing in entrances of
stores and theaters along Broadway ...
where junkies shoot up casually,
climbing over each other naturally
as patrons continue on,
hypnotically dodging casualties,

the dreamers in the Gulag
of the U.S.A
lose themselves in visions
of life without hassles
for shelter every day ...

there's dreamers hanging out
in the neon nights of America today ...
lounging on street corners
in cities,
wandering the sidewalks of towns,
drifting through alleyways

blowing smoke rings at
the screens of scenes seen
while floating away
from
the streets of yesterday ...

****

"What It Was Like"

****

San Francisco, California 1963-64-65 was a mad Zen bike ride on the Great Highway, El Camino Real, The King's Highway. From San Mateo to Marin, we did it in a day, the Great Escape of a run away.

There were so many runaways in those days ... kids hanging out in North Beach, Sausalito, the Waterfront, Gate 5 Road. Working at Juanita's Galley for tips. Wandering the streets of Bridgeway, walking across the Orange Bridge to Grant Avenue, to hang out again in Washington Square Park, or Mike's Place on Broadway, to wander past the Hot Dog Palace, to cross the street to Columbus, to go into the City Lights Bookstore, across the alley from Vesuvio's.

We would go to the park, to the bookstore, to the donut shop, but we couldn't go to the bars, with names like the Anxious Asp, the Capri, the Coffee Gallery ... we couldn't go to the places where only drinks were served, but we could go to the Spaghetti Factory, to the laundromat, to the grocery store. We could go to Coit Tower, to the poolroom, to the 24-hour delicatessen in Sausalito, the Kettle, with murals on the walls. It was one of our favorite places, along with the Tides Book Store on Bridgeway. We didn't like to drink coffee; we just got high on the aroma ... and some of the older people there were teacher types who walked around smoking pipes. Those two aromas ... coffee and pipe smoke ... were like middle-class incense to us, the runaway college dropouts.

What it was like: Coming from San Francisco, that's

where it all began. City Lights and Lenny Bruce, free LSD, Electric Kool Aid, the ultimate acid test, Flower Power, the Summer of Love, the Grateful Dead and the Diggers too ... yeah ...

Coming from San Francisco, the City by the Bay, two bridges, three islands, a rainbow tunnel up from Wolf Back Ridge, above Sausalito. We called it Never Never Land many years ago, even before the psychedelic cycle began ... Janis Joplin sang on Grant Avenue in the Coffee Gallery before she was famous, and Mario Savio spoke there in 1965, just a couple of years after Kennedy died. There was a sign on the bathroom door: "Please Don't Shoot Up Inside" ... and just down the street another bartender had gotten busted and the place called the Greenspot was closed down. The heroin traffic was just too heavy; suddenly there were cops all around, all the users had to go underground.

Coming from San Francisco, that's my hometown. In the beginning, 1961, everything was beautiful; everything was young and full of wonder ... but then in 1968, the Haight turned into a dreadful place; a concentration camp atmosphere smothered the space ... it became a ghetto of poor crazy speed freaks, all alone, hanging out, rushing the dealer's car. All the doors were locked as we cruised the avenues. There weren't any more free handouts. Everyone was high, and the desolate adolescents who'd come from everywhere were freaking out on sidewalks, clothes flapping crazily, bodies filthy, eyes dazed and glassy, hair matted and lousy. The Hippie Childrens' Concentration Camp Blues had just begun, and was continuing ...

1978, a decade later, the heat busted again ... all

over the city, there was nothing to be found; everyone was dry, scouring the underground. Skid row depression hung in the air.

On Sixth Street, Wino Park was built, and then a decade later closed down. Too many "expensive" winos and junkies hanging around, all over the sidewalks, all over the town, too many derelicts to be found.

In 1988, we see another side of society; cocaine, the ultimate drug of mind control, has taken its place in the pharmacy of fame. Crack cocaine, the Third World train, blue rock's gotten out of control, people on the street selling poison just to fill their pockets with gold, and the heat is busting before the corpses turn too cold ... while the prisons are bursting and the parents are crying that their babies are having their civil rights broken. The issue is pain versus medicine; the users get beaten 'cause the system's out of control.

Politicians are corrupt and the devil's buying souls ... we've got to move 'cause this train's rushing through these pages of another soul's journey, over tracks of black and blue with little bits of red shining through, tracks with blood and lines of white powder, through smoke curls of "M" and "O", another soul's journey is ready to roll. After the bottles and needles, after the blotter, the tabs and the cottons, after the pills and ODs, after the prayers and miraculous mysteries, another story's waiting to be told ... so let the tale unfold ...

****

"Los Angeles: 1950s"

****

I'll never forget the time my grandparents took me to Hollywood to see Disneyland. It was horrible. I hated it because I could hardly breathe due to the smog.

The smog in L.A. burns your eyes on a hot summer day. If you're stuck in a car on the freeway you can't open the windows for fresh air, but must depend on the air conditioning system inside. The smog was so thick it looked like fog, but fog is misty, damp, cleansing. Smog is dirty and suffocating, the result of billions of particles of carbon monoxide from the exhaust systems of millions of cars ... and like it says in somebody's song, L.A. is just one big freeway.

The landscape outside the car windows is monotonous after you've seen it once; it's always the same ... the same pattern of houses, trees and freeway for miles and miles. Malvina Reynolds wrote a song about a similar phenomenon of duplication in San Francisco, and called it "Little Boxes On A Hillside". The song was popular in the 1960s, and was about the similarity of people who live in similar tract houses, have similar educations and lifestyles with similar backgrounds, aspirations, hopes and beliefs.

We also stopped at a Knott's Berry Farm on the trip. That's a big deal in California. From Sacramento to L.A. there are hundreds of Knott's Berry Farms along the way. Most of California is new, relatively speaking. New tile, formica, porcelain, aluminum, the houses, the schools, the restaurants. Things in California are also big compared to the three hundred year old buildings and streets that you can find in the Great Northeast, where the states are so close together that skipping from one to the other can sometimes be as easy as going from town to town.

The culture of the Eastern seaboard is filled with concentrated pockets, while that of California is homogenized. Due to the public school system and the fast food industry, different nationalities become assimilated almost instantly.

****

"San Mateo County, California: 1956"

****

Over forty years ago in San Mateo County, my parents were in a community play together, a work by Tennessee Williams called "Summer and Smoke". My mother acted one of the parts and my father made the Angel for the set. It was a life-sized wooden Angel, standing on a pedestal like the Statue of Liberty. The play was successful, and after it finished its run the Angel was retired to my father's studio, a recycled barn in the back yard of the house. I used to do my freshman year high school homework at the feet of this Angel. I did my first English term paper, on the religious aspects of the newly emerging Beat literary movement, in the barn, under the eyes of the Angel.

The activity of these few chaps had been highly publicized in the local press and national magazines, resulting in an increased interest in poetry both in the schools and in the general population. My paper reflected that interest, drawing parallels between the concrete poetry of John Donne and Thomas Carew and the concrete poetry of representative San Francisco poets. I got a B+ on the assignment.

At that time we were poverty-stricken, although it didn't seem that way. We lived in a house on a grassy knoll in a small peninsula town in Northern California, some twenty miles outside of San Francisco. I'd walk to and from the high school every day, carrying my books, just like all the other kids did. But every night I'd take a quarter from my father's suit coat pocket, which was in the closet near their bed, next to the bathroom. If my parents woke up and caught me doing this, I'd planned to say that I'd stumbled into the closet by mistake. It was dark; a groggy person could easily make this error. But they never woke up, so I never had to say this.

Having obtained the quarter after they were asleep, I'd run across the highway, El Camino Real, to the newly opened 19-cent hamburger drive-in and get a burger. At that time they were razor-thin gray circles pressed into a bun, with a single slice of onion underneath the patty on top of a single knife-blade spread of mayonnaise. This bit of protein was wrapped in a non-waxed paper, and two small slices of butter pickles were usually placed under the paper on top of the bun. Having secured this food, I would run back across the highway to the room in the back that I had as my own. After eating, I would take the lamp, the radio and my school papers and notebook out to the barn and do my homework under the silent wooden gaze of my father's Angel.

This was freshman year, the year my mother flipped. The nervous breakdown she experienced is described on other pages. Perhaps she knew that I was taking that quarter every night from my father's pocket. I had to do it, though, because I had to be able to think properly to do my homework. My brothers were always eating all the food that came into the house in one fell swoop, like a bunch of starving vultures. After all, they were growing boys, and were doing what they could to assure their own survival.

Earlier, in South San Francisco, we used to make tea from mint leaves and cobbler from the blackberries growing in the hobo jungle by the train tracks, down the hill from the projects at the end of the street. When we moved to the new house in San Bruno on Santa Maria Avenue, these little grammar school rituals were gone. There was a store at the end of the block, but we hardly ever had any money to spend there. That was when I asked for a job at the high school cafeteria. It was a 50 cents an hour gig for a half hour every lunch time, but I had to wait until my junior year to get it because my mother had another nervous breakdown in the meantime.

This time our family was torn asunder. I went to Immaculate Conception Academy in San Francisco, a Catholic boarding school operated by the Sisters of Mercy, and my brothers and sisters were sent to other Catholic boarding schools in Ukiah and San Raphael. When my mother came back from the hospital and I was returned to her, we used to go on horrible all-day weekend trips to visit my brothers and sisters in their various boarding schools. We'd all get carsick from riding four to five hours up and four to five hours back from the Peninsula to Ukiah or San Raphael ... or both ... on a Sunday. We'd start out in the morning after Mass, and not return until the evening. Having to get ready to go back to school again after these trips was another hassle, as I had to get the remaining brothers and sisters ready also, since Mother would be in the midst of yet another pregnancy.

My mother was finally told that she'd have diabetes if she had another pregnancy. When she told my father, he said, "Well, then, that's the end of the marriage." Of course, my father denies to this day ever having said such a thing. Neither one of them seem to remember very much. It's just as well they don't. We remember more than they do about these times, as children often will.

I don't believe that the marriage vows mean "in sickness and in health" only for the man. When a woman's life is at stake, isn't her husband to stand by her? When the Catholic Church encourages the family to have children, I don't think this means at the expense of the mother's health, which is the way some people interpret it. I don't think the good fathers or God want to have the women die or conract illness due to childbirth. I don't think the higher powers believe that the female is expendible and that the male of the species is the only supreme being. We have a long ways to go yet before reaching divinity if we use women's bodies only as though they were storage bins for the birthing of babies.

Over these chaotic years I went to five different high schools, but still managed to graduate on time in 1961. After that I was going to the College of San Mateo and taking bacteriology, working as a waitress at a Borden's Fountain in Burlingame after class. I'd put my paycheck in the bank and give my mother the tips.

When I could get away with it, I'd give my brothers and sisters free food from the Fountain when they came in. I'd say that it was the food I wasn't eating on my break. By that time I'd been hospitalized with nephritis and was allergic to large amounts of protein ... all kidney patients are.

Over time, the money in the bank grew and grew until at last I had enough to rent my own place, which I did, moving out secretly one night. When I started college, my parents had moved to a house in San Mateo across from where I attended class, but I didn't have a room there in which to do my homework. Bacteriology is a complex science course, and one needs somewhere to do the homework, other than the bottom half of a bunk in a room with three other very active kids, or the formica table of a restaurant during break-time. I couldn't do it at the library; I was working at the Fountain during the hours that the library was open. But I was a seventeen-year-old girl, and when the decision was made to change our living arrangements, no one would listen to my side of the story. Even though I had specific needs, it was as if I was a non-person, swept along in the tide of events controlled by others.

So, as soon as I was able, I took the saved money and rented a place in Burlingame a block up from the library. I climbed out the window one night and went over to the new place, making several trips through the silent midnight streets with my paltry belongings until finally I was moved in. My family didn't know where I was living until one of my brothers followed me home one day and then went back and told my mother and father. That was Tony.

He hasn't fared too well in this life since then. These days he lives alone in a trailer, does odd jobs, takes medication and writes about being pursued by "brain demons" in a manuscript called "Return To Ithaca" that he has sent me to read. It's about a boy who drives his girlfriend to suicide while they are patients in a mental hospital. That's the gist of the story that I was able to ascertain when I read it.

****

"Aftermath: 1961-1963"

****

Shortly after my seventeenth birthday, and my exit from the family home, the County decided to tell my poor mother that they could no longer keep her growing family, and that she didn't earn enough to keep them herself according to their standards. They were going to terminate the supplemental AFDC check, and she would either have to move or have her children taken away from her. How many mothers with ten children can find a place to live without any money? No one ... hardly anyone.

My mother went up to Sacramento where her mother and stepfather lived and told them what the County had told her. Her stepfather told her to look around for a house and he'd buy it for her. She did, and in 1961, my mother and her remaining children moved to the house in Butte County which is still her home today. However, her stepfather had bought her the house under the provision that my father, her husband, never live there. What could a poor woman with ten children do? She took the offer and moved to the house that was provided.

My father then finally did for himself what he'd never fully done for us ... he took care of himself. He got a job as a security guard in San Francisco, and paid his own bills out of the money he earned. Why couldn't he have done that before? Only heaven knows. Of course, if he had, things would have been different.

My brothers Jimmy, Tony, Christopher, Philip, Andy and Peter would have had a legitimate fatherly role model to follow. My sisters Mari-Beth, Veronica, Kathy and Sylvia would have had a father they could talk about as other girls talked about theirs. But perhaps the madness, brutality,starvation and insanity were all meant to be. These are the side effects of war. When this happened to my family the war in Europe was long over, but the carryover in the States was apparently just beginning.

While my mother was getting newly situated in the house on Pomona Avenue in 1961, I was living in foster care in San Mateo and eventually ran away with a friend to Sausalito on our bicycles, where we stayed overnight on an empty houseboat with the intention of finding the owner the next day and renting if from him. We did, and then rode back down to the Peninsula to pack up our cares and woes into our backpacks, turn our bikes around and head on back to Sausalito. Of course this mad Zen bike ride took place before the emergence of the hippies, but not before the use of LSD.

The first time I saw anyone on LSD was at my foster parents' home in 1962. One of their friends, a college professor with a Doctorate in Theology from Stanford University in Palo Alto, California arrived for a weekend visit on LSD, which doctors had prescribed to help him with his alcoholism. Previously he'd been dismissed from tenure at the local junior college for an alleged indiscretion with one of his students.

... Just took a break from all this writing to put on my protections, my gems and jewels: tiger's eye, jade, rose quartz, rainbow crystal, mother of pearl, carnelian, amythest and moonstone ... these gems were among the first medicines, now recognized in holistic and Buddhist circles. I'm also dieting because of my kidneys, the nephritis which makes me unable to assimilate concentrated nutrients ... that's also the price of alcoholism, methamphetamine addiction and miscellaneous consumption of numerous doses of white lightning and tabs of LSD.

Perhaps I have ulcers. Living under stress for as many years as I have could ruin anyone's digestive system.

****

"My Father and My Mother"

****

One night over the phone my father told me that in a previous lifetime he had been a swordmaker in a 13th century castle in France. Once he gave my brother Tony and me a pair of fencing foils, one for each of us. We sold them to an antique dealer rather then use them on each other. Now, in the latter 1990s, my father works on models of carousel horses and paintings he hasn't finished yet in his studio in San Francisco. It's in a stucco house in the Sunset district out by the Great Highway. There's a small Italian garden in the back and a picture window in the front, with a rounded staircase leading up to the door.

My father was in the second African invasion during the Second World War as a private in the Army Corps of Engineers. When these troops landed, they had to clear the airstrip of the bodies of all the soldiers who had taken part in the first African invasion. The suddenness of such total immersion in death left a devastating impression upon my father's psyche.

Apparently his spiritual desolation after this experience was not an isolated phenomenom. According to a 1985 article in the Journal of Community Psychology, almost all the soldiers in the North African Theater in 1943 who were not physically disabled or wounded became neuropsychiatric casualties. The problem was so bad that the number of casualties recorded even exceeded the number of men involved, as many of them suffered multiple incidences of psychiatric distress upon their return to civilian life.

He was a distant father to me, but a close disciplinarian. He taught me how to play chess so that I would know how to think. We would stay up at night playing after the rest of the family had gone to bed. Once on one of our walks through San Francisco's Chinatown he told me never to look into people's eyes while walking along the sidewalks.

The other night during a phone call my mother told me of a secret tragedy she'd lived with most of her life. When she was a child during the 1920s, after her mother had divorced her father, she had been sent to live with her mother's sister and her husband, her aunt and uncle. One night, my mother heard the two of them arguing over the $50.00 a month that her mother was paying them for her keep. The uncle wanted his wife to give him that money. She said no, that the money had been given to her for Mary Jane's care and was to be spent on her needs. My mother told me that a few nights later the uncle came to her room while she was in bed and touched her in places on her body in ways that made her feel bad.

She said that he told her that if she told anyone about it he would deny it and that she wouldn't be able to live there anymore. When she did try to tell her mother what was happening to her in the evenings at the home of their relatives, her mother said that she didn't believe her and told her she'd better stop making up lies such as that. Her mother just couldn't allow herself to listen and comprehend. She had nowhere else to board this child of her first marriage, a single mother on limited resources with a child she had to provide for as best she could in those unsettled times.

For over seventy years my mother had kept this early assault to herself, but the results of it were manifested in other ways. Such an early exposure, with such horrible unresolved consequences, caused her hurt to grow. When she had children of her own, and a husband of her own, the unresolved assault that had happened may have been the catalyst for her later reactions to the situations of poverty and frustration that she faced.

So now, after all this time, I come upon the possible reasons for the beatings, the starvation, the replication of war in my household in front of my eyes at the hands of my parents. It was a sort of gigantic psychodrama being enacted by my father and mother to help resolve their own devastating life experiences.

My parents were married in 1942, after my father proposed to my mother at Coit Tower, that steeple of the North Beach community which rises as a beacon above the legendary beat streets of Upper Grant Avenue. I was born in 1943, and it has taken me over fifty years to discover some of the reasons behind the madness and brutality of those early years, triggered by the frustrations of war and poverty.

"Life at Home: 1953"

We used to go to church every Sunday morning as a family. My job was to get the younger children ready for Mass, as my mother was always either pregnant or in the process of recovering from a pregnancy. The nervous breakdowns she experienced later on in her life were a result of the malnutrition caused by these continuous pregnancies taking place in the midst of poverty.

The 1950s when I grew up was an era that offered little help. There were no food stamps, WIC programs, community health centers or sympathetic social workers that I could remember. The country was in a state of terror. Television was rapidly becoming a household item, and the McCarthy trials were broadcast daily and highlighted on the noon and evening news.

I remember as a kid coming home from school at 4 or

5 o'clock to watch the Howdy Doody show and the Mouseketeers. In the morning we would watch Crusader Rabbit, and on Saturday evenings there was the Hit Parade, and then at midnight the Owl Theater.

On family outings we usually went for a picnic to the bandshell in Golden Gate Park, where a concert was performed by an orchestra all afternoon. We'd sit on the green benches and eat our bananas, rye bread and velveeta cheese or peanut butter sandwiches to the rhythm of Strauss waltzes, Chopin mazurkas, John Philip Sousa marches and Gershwin's Rhapsody in Blue. After lunch we'd wander around in the trees and saunter over to the Aquarium and Planetarium which were in big white marble buildings across the roadway. We'd have to climb stairs to get there.

Later, when I grew up, I'd go to the Japanese Tea Garden across the road from the bandshell, and wander around on the bridges there looking at all the delicate flowers and the lily pads floating on the leaf-strewn waters under the Oriental structures. I'd sit on the round wooden seats at one of the picnic tables and drink jasmine tea, with delicate almond rice cakes on the side, and remember the family picnics of yesteryear ... they showed us where to run to ...

One day, instead of the usual trip to the park, my parents took us for a ride in their old black Lincoln to North Beach. They wanted to renew their memories and revisit some of their old haunts. They'd often gone to the Black Cat and the Iron Pot when my father was a student at the San Francisco Art Institute and my mother modeled there. So they drove up in front of the newly-opened City Lights Bookstore and told me and my brother Jimmy to get out and go exploring, that they would come back and pick us up in a couple of hours.

We got out, went down the alley next to the bookstore and wandered along the sidewalks of Chinatown, marveling at the strangeness of the place ... the aromas, the architecture, the mysterious things in the shops, such as dried ducks hanging upside down in the windows. Jimmy and I went up to Stockton Street to the opening of the Tunnel and walked back down till we reached the Fu dogs guarding the entrance to Chinatown. We climbed up on them and rode them for awhile, until the shadows of dusk reminded us of our parents.

When we returned to the alley and saw that their car wasn't there, we went into the bookstore. Climbing the winding, narrow staircase to the little room on the second floor, we watched for the car through the windows. While we were waiting, I played a few tunes on my recorder and Jimmy looked for pictures in the books. Nobody told us to be quiet. When we saw the car pull up, we left.

Years later when I was on my own, City Lights was one of the places that I'd go. It was just the right size for a teenage scholar, and the fact that it was open till midnight made it a perfect sanctuary in the hours before I entered the North Beach nightlife through the doors of the Hot Dog Palace and other places.

****

"Growing Up In Northern California"

****

The bruises spoke for themselves, the black and blue

told the story of the beatings, the welts of purple hue that took forever to fade away, giant swollen welts on arms, legs and back, made with fists and belts, made with spatulas and rubber hoses, made with broom and mop sticks, with two by fours and hammer grips, anything that came to hand ... anything within reach of those mad, brutalized, brutalizing love-starved hands ... both parents participated in such punishings.

The bruises spoke for themselves, to the gym teacher who asked, "Where'd you get those marks?", as though soliciting your confidence, foolishly thinking that a kid with marks like that would ever again trust any adult ... and so you'd say your brothers had beaten you up, that you had six brothers, which was true, and that you'd fight with each other a lot, and that was where the marks had come from. Finally I ran away.

I tried to do it professionally, with a job and an apartment, but I hadn't anticipated the reaction of the oppressor ... the mother who spied on me, who called the cops on me, and the vice squad and the social workers, saying I was this, that and the other thing ... and so she had me busted by the agents of control for being too young to be ... I was ordered to a local orphanage, and then a foster home.

Eventually when I was a little older and had figured out the routine of county government and developed a plan of escape I moved three counties away, knowing that the disinterested arm of the law would not bother to stretch that far to reach out for me. When I was twenty-one I left the state completely, heading East to a land of snow and ice that I had not seen since

I was three. Now, looking back on that time from a distance of thirty-some-odd years, it doesn't seem that long ago or far away. It's more like yesterday.

When I open the windows of my mind, gazing down the corridors of time I see other people have been there before me. Charlie Chaplin was a poor boy too ... the Tramp that charmed the world with a rose ... and Edith Piaf with her sister too, they sang for change on the streets of Paris until Jean Cocteau declared her to be quite a catch ... Jean Genet did his best writing from a prison cell ... if not locked up, he used other pastimes to occupy his days, doing things he'd learned in the orphanages, reformatories and foster homes he'd gone through ... Billie Holliday, Louis Armstrong, Charlie Parker ... all children of poverty who gave much to the world of music despite their early lack of money ...

Daniel Patrick Moynihan, United States Senator today, came from the streets of Hell's Kitchen in New York City, and James Baldwin sprang up out of Harlem, with its slum landlords preying on the destitute whenever they may ... and Jesus was a poor boy ... his mother Mary knows, on that first birthday they had no place to stay ... had to share space with the animals in a stable on that first Christmas day ... so the story goes ...

****

"Jazz, All That Jazz: 1963-1977"

****

Jazz, child of the cities, of the projects, of the joints, the pool halls, tenements, railroad flats, walkup apartments ... jazz, the sound of the soul blowing its guts out into the night, the sound of the soul crying tears of notes to the sky, the sound of the soul talking to the breeze, running with the wind, lighting the fires within ...

Jazz, dancing with the trees, prancing in the rain, making melody after melody to ease the pain, sounding through the lane ... Cooper Lane, 39 Cooper Lane ... where the Tin Angel sighed when her soul flew into the sky, and her body died ... she told me she was the first one to put jazz on the San Francisco Embarcadero ... Dixeland jazz played in her club, the nightclub in the lot underneath Coit Tower ... Kid Ory, trombone man from New Orleans, bought the club from her, and Turk Murphy, who once worked there, has his own place on the Embarcadero, now called Earthquake MaGoon's ... they rock it nightly with a jamboree underneath the Harbor, underneath the moon, down the street from Fat Ron's jukebox saloon ...

Listen to the sounds, low, cool, mellow, blue-gold swing, swaying round/flat/sharp, whole subtle rings ... of trumpet, sax, trombone, clarinet, flute notes floating all around ... oh, what a 14-year trip it's been, from the shooting galleries and rock emporiums of the 60s through the progressive backlash of the '70s ... of nuthouses and electric kool-aid acid tests, where more than one flew over the cuckoo's nest, to go on the road again and again ... via car, train, airplane, bus, pickup truck, back and forth across this glorious land, to trip and trip, again and again ...

Oh, what a trip, all those years spent following the sound of the piper, the song of the sage ... we heard the melody playing in our minds, leading us away, away from suburbia, away from the tract houses and the colleges ... the sound of the sax, of the flute, of the trumpet, of the recorder, of the bamboo pipes, leading us to the city sidewalks, the all-night restaurants, the bookstores, leading us through the streets of Chinatown, beckoning to us from the lanes, the alleys, the hidden places of the metropolis ...

****

"39 Cooper Lane"

****

This was my off-and-on official address from November 1963 until April 1971, when I left to go and sit in the Kettle in the early morning hours and write. My brother Tony was working there as chief chef, cook and bottle washer for Leo Krekorien, one of Peggy's old colleagues from Black Mountain College. Tony worked the graveyard shift from 9 p.m. to 5 a.m., making soup, selling coffee, beer, sandwiches, whatever else.

He scrubbed the big pots used to make the 50-cent lentil soup, scrubbed the coffee urn and cleaned the inside of the delicatessen refrigerator -- hard labor! He mopped the floor and cleaned off the tables, locked up the joint and then made it on up to Cooper Lane, where Peggy let him stay in a room at the house in exchange for the nightly sandwich that she lived on, supplemented with burgundy.

I lived there in 1969 with Tony and Peggy. I typed my ever-growing manuscripts, went to the store, cooked for Peggy occasionally and painted the interior of the upstairs apartment black and white at her request in exchange for rent. I'd sun myself on the roof and listen to the neighbors splashing around in their swimming pool while Peggy was crashed out in her bed. Her life, from the streets of Brooklyn to the classrooms of Black Mountain, the housing projects of Richmond to the neighborhoods of San Francisco and Sausalito, had left her exhausted, wasted, beat. Peggy was a poet and a painter, a mother and a nightclub owner, an entrepreneur, an operator, a godmother and a comedian, a tragic clown. She was rough, she was tough, and had been built to last ... she's lasted in my mind for over thirty years.

She read e.e. cummings to me with feeling, encouraged my music, and forced me to talk, using a dialectic method of telling me a story and then asking me to tell me what she said in my own words. I was nineteen years old and no one had ever asked me what I thought about anything to such an extent before ... those sessions in front of the fireplace were grueling to me. I wasn't used to thinking. My life had been so active that I'd primarily learned to react.

****

"San Francisco, 1971"

****

We were living on the street, having fun, hanging out, writing poetry in the Kettle on Bridgeway in Sausalito. I'd just decided to leave that house with all the haunted silences, all the tattered publicity on the wall and my friend's exhausted body lying wasted from her life. When my fellowship at MacDowell Colony was over, I'd gotten drunk on everyone else's liquor and gone to New York City to make it as a writer.

After two weeks of that I left town, at two o'clock in the morning from the Port Authority, with two dollars in my pocket, Willard's admonitions in my head, a bottle of brandy in my bag and a pocket full of shattered dreams.

I hadn't been able to adjust to the "straight" world after being a flower child for a couple of fateful years in San Francisco and Marin County. During 1968 I'd spent nine months shooting methamphetamine with friends three times a day, and then three months smoking opium to get over it. Countless hits of LSD had managed to disrupt whatever conditioning and socialization I'd acquired while wandering through thirteen years of Northern California's public school system. The indoctrination of those pre-drugged years had been dissolved and scattered throughout my psyche as are the images of a kalaidescope when the cylinder is turned.

****

"How I Met Willard"

****

On an afternoon in 1966 in Saratoga Springs, New York, I was sitting on the green carpet at Lena's house when I heard my name called. Lena wanted to introduce me to someone. I got up, wandered into the gigantic ballroom-sized living room with its wall of windows and there was Lena, sitting at the table with an older gentleman of scholarly appearance. As I approached, she said, "Willard, this is Bria!". Turning to me, she said, "Bria, I'd like you to meet Willard Trask!"

I took the hand extended to me and nodded my head, not really knowing what was expected of me in relation to this grandfatherly chap. He wasn't as flashy as Johnny, better known as John Wynn Evans, the Caffe's acting troupe director. But he was there, and I was expected to meet him, though I didn't know why. Apparently Lena did typing for Willard, who was staying at the artists' colony Yaddo while working on volumes of literature for which he had a deadline. I was in my early twenties and a fugitive, who'd been taken in by the Caffe Lena Players one December night in 1965 because my clothes could be used as costumes for their plays. Willard had translated many books by the French metaphysician Mirceau Eliade, books about religion, yoga and immortality.

He'd also translated audiotapes of spoken songs collected from primitive peoples on Earth today, those who still pass their culture on from one generation to the next by word of mouth. These were sung by people on the run: Pygmies, Polynesians and other African and Australian hunter/gatherers, songs for courting, songs of love and death, of God and in praise of the earth, its elements and seasons.

I never forgot Willard Trask from the day we met at Lena's in Saratoga in 1966 until 1980, when he died of a heart attack one evening while dining with his lawyer in New York City. He was an emissary from an American literary tradition that's rapidly fading away to non-existence. Willard was from the world of e.e.cummings, Marianne Moore, Carson McCullers, Truman Capote, Ford Maddox Ford, Ernest Hemingway, F. Scott Fitzgerald, Josephine Herbst, John Dos Passos, Dorothy Parker and Gertrude Stein. He'd danced with Anna Pavlova when he was fourteen And his father was an engineer on the

Panama Canal. Over the years he encouraged my artistic endeavors spiritually and concretely, both face to face and in numerous letters and postcards.

The last time I saw Willard was in Saratoga Springs in 1977. He pointed out the Winged Statue of Life to me in Congress Park. This statue reminded me of my father's Angel from so many years before. At that time Willard told me that if anything ever happened to jeopardize my living situation in Saratoga, I should go out to Yaddo and take sanctuary on the grounds there to get me through to the next day ...

A few months later, while the Caffe Lena Players were performing the "Spoon River Anthology", the room I had in the boardinghouse across the street was gutted by flames. It was an accidental grease fire started by another tenant cooking porkchops on a hotplate in his room down the hall. Everything was destroyed.

Earlier that day I'd almost gotten a sleep inducing herb from the local health food store to help me fight insomnia. I decided to go to the play instead, and ended up watching the flames from the Caffe windows rather than sleeping through the incident on my way to a fiery death. As the evening got later and I no longer had a place to stay, I remembered Willard's words and wandered out to Yaddo, finding a piece of material along the way. That cloth became my cover as I slept safely in the leaves until the following day.

Of course I miss Willard and will always acknowledge the impact he had on my life. He was the most elegant, sentient, sophisticated man I ever met.

****

"Living on Lemonade and Other Things"

****

I've never put this down on paper before, how I was living on sugar, lemons and water from July to December 1977 after the fire in my apartment across from the Caffe. I was staying at the Orange Blossom Inn in Ballston Spa, surviving on lemonade until I had to stop, because the pain of such little sustenance became unbearable. To pay my rent, I created a music studio for the drummer who lived downstairs, and also loaded up and brought in twelve boxes of wood a day, six for him and six for me, to heat the house. We had wood stoves, me upstairs and him downstairs. On weekends we would drive into town to the Caffe, where I'd work in the kitchen for a portion of the tips to supplement my meager income, $200.00 a month from disability.

At the time my front teeth were broken and no one in mainstream society would hire me, not even for a waitress job. Luckily, there was the Caffe. Before the fire, in my room across from the Caffe, I'd kept nonfat dry milk, sugar, teabags and hot chocolate as my food supply. Undomiciled men, guided by John Wynn Evans, the acting troupe's director, would come to my room and sit and talk for hours, drinking up all my tea and hot chocolate. John was conducting this event because Lena, the Caffe owner, was mad at him at the time.

One night I got him to read the dialogue of a primitive tribe called the Tasaday with me while pretending we were members of a Stone Age family. The words of this tribe reminded me of the hippies' life-style in San Francisco during the 1960s. After the reading we made audiotapes of these words. Eventually, Lena forgave John for whatever it was that had caused her to be mad at him and things returned to normal.

John liked my piano harp music, which he'd heard from tapes I'd made while wandering around the town, stopping to play the disgarded instrument whereever I might find one. This instrument consisted of the sounding board and inner strings -- the bare music-making components -- of a standard piano. At that time I was playing one such pianoharp left on the porch of the Hilwin House, a stately, white-columned building on Caroline Street; the other which I also played was in back of a house at the end of what is now called Lena Lane.

I played these instruments by plucking melodies on the inner strings with my fingernails, and occasionally running an open palm across all the strings, from the lowest part of the bass clef to the highest notes in the treble. The resulting crescendo of sound was volcanic, as though an avalance of notes had suddenly escaped the wood to roam the environment.

After Lena and John made up, he did his play, "All Day For a Dollar", at the Caffe and asked me to do the music for the entrance, intermission and end of the show. It was a very sad story about a derelict who worked at slave labor all day for a dollar. John played the primary part, of the derelict. I think the play was about his friend Duncan Gillespie, who'd lived in the back room of the Caffe Lena for years while being the organist of an area church. The show ran for two weeks, with 14 performances. Reluctantly, Lena included my name on the program.

She'd never forgiven me for checking myself into a mental hospital after being lauded as a writer at the MacDowell Colony. She couldn't understand why I was sick in 1976, and not able to drink and smoke as I had in 1966 and '67. Lena was very "old world" in some of her attitudes, whimsical and practical and magical, rather like Laura in the Tennessee Williams play, The Glass Managerie, with a dash of the Caffe owner in The Rose Tattoo thrown in for good measure.

Lena can never be replaced She was the Caffe. We never thought she'd die ... she was always so strong, so responsible! At least it seemed that way to us, the artists she looked out for, as might a mother for her children.

****

"1991: Albany Reflections"

****

As I peruse the TV channels in my mind, a picture emerges of a foggy day that casts a curtain of mist over the contents of a village of wooden, brick and granite structures. A closer focus reveals thin sheets of rain drifting through the mid-morning, down onto the streets and sidewalks of this quaint North American, "All American" Eastern town.

The capital of New York State presents an unpretentious facade to the world that comes to see her. The agency buildings adorning the Empire State Plaza are similar in function to computer chips, and aerial views of the city would confirm the visual resemblance. These state buildings are the paper factories of this present-day city. The laws, licenses, regulations, records, cases, litigations and other legal matters of the state are all decided and stored in Albany, New York.

For years this word was just a name in a folk song to me ... "We were thirty miles from Albany on the Erie Canal ... " and then suddenly, quite unexpectedly, I landed here ten years ago in January 1981, the start of the Reagan Era, the beginning of the freeze.

The winters here are bitter. Temperatures drop to zero and below, the snow freezes and we walk on sheets of ice with tiny steps and a prayer on every breath. The winters last for six months; the air is crisp, and sometimes takes your breath away. It's very easy to die in Albany, to contract pneumonia or T.B., to get frostbite when the cold just suddenly is. It's hard to stay alive and maintain physical health: you have to work at it.

Winter seems to have started early this year. In the decade of the 1980s, there was a blizzard in October. The streets of Albany were buried in dunes of snow, tree limbs were torn from their trunks. Cars skidded along the highways, to eventually stop, and then they were lined up, one after the other along the curb, their owners long gone, looking for a tow truck or some place to wait out the weather. Cars were suddenly a liability, dysfunctional nonessential items in the stark environment.

In a blizzard it's difficult to see; the air is full of blinding whiteness, a whiteness that stings and cuts into exposed flesh, coldness that tears through the layers of insulation you might be wearing. Eventually, if you're out in the cold long enough, your faculties become numbed, your state of being is that of an organism existing in an environment of pain alternating with spots of warmth. Perhaps your gloves aren't warm enough for zero degrees or below ... the feeling goes from the tips of your fingers ... at such times you'd better do something, or you could lose your hands or feet or nose or ears from frostbite.

It's very easy to get sick in Albany, easy to die, if one wants to. During the long winter months, there's always the possibility that if things become unbearable you can always contract pneumonia and not recover. There's always that possibility! The same amount of chance exists as that experienced by a junkie who scores on the street. He never knows when the next shot might be the last. Such challenges make life bearable in this age of death trips.

I've been in Albany, New York since January 1981. When I came here from San Francisco I had only the clothes on my back, as my suitcase had been delayed for two weeks by the bus company. I didn't have the proper clothes for the show ... I didn't have the proper shoes! Since that time I've had numerous bouts with pneumonia, but I don't get it any more. I almost died from it in 1986. It terrified me, that particular event. But it wasn't time for me to go yet. I had to give up smoking instead. Finally I just got sick of getting a sore throat and losing my voice, so I changed my lifestyle in order to avoid such things.

Now I have a job in which there is incentive not to use your sick leave, as it can turn into vacation time if allowed to accumulate. In this age of computer-ization and information revolution, time is of the essence as there is so little of it free. Perhaps in the future there will be more leisure, days for thinking, writing, being ... but at this stage of my life, I find that there's just not enough time for personal pursuits.

Right now I'm between classes, having just finished the second summer session, waiting for fall semester to start. Meanwhile, I find myself at the job with nothing to do and no personal leave or vacation days that I can take off.

Sometimes the office I work in is very busy and sometimes it's almost dead, especially on cold, wet, rainy days such as this one, or in the winter when the snow begins to fall. People usually don't like to go out in such weather, preferring to stay in a warm environment. This is only natural. That's probably why the warmer states in America are so full of people while the colder states are losing population.

Eventually the majority of the people of North America might redistribute themselves throughout the warmer areas, and we in the East will have more space ...

****

"Saratoga, 1967: Willard"

****

Willard came up to me one day while I was sweeping out the Caffe and announced that one of his translations, "Memoirs of Casanova", had won the National Book Award of 1967. I was in a "sans culotte" mode and couldn't understand why he was telling me of this. I was listening to Bobby Dylan songs, and active in the revolution that was rapidly changing the face of America while rearranging the Establishment.

Willard, to me, was obviously part of the Establishment. I was engaged in very physical, hard work, cleaning up the Caffe after every show, stacking the chairs on top of the tables, sweeping the floors and then mopping them, wiping off the tables, going to the store, to the post office, the newspaper office, making posters advertising the current act. I was all of 23 years old, and needed approximately 1530 calories to accomplish these tasks and have enough energy left over to do my painting and other personal activities, such as dancing in the clubs on the other side of town in Saratoga. I had it all figured out.

Then Willard started coming to my studio on the top floor of the Hilwin House. He'd walk the three miles or so from Yaddo with bits of his lunch that he'd saved to share with me. At the time my daily routine started off each morning with burgundy, switching to brandy at about two o'clock in the afternoon. This would carry me through the rest of the day, until the next morning, when I'd start off with burgundy again.

This diet came to an abrupt end one day when Willard took my bottle away from me, the day I was asked to leave my own 24th birthday party after insulting one of the newly arrived, older female guests attending the celebration because of her dress and the pronounced cleavage that she exhibited at what ws supposed to be my occasion.

I swore at him that evening as he went running down the long, winding circular balcony staircase of the Hilwin House. He'd left me just an inch of brandy in a crystal glass. I cried myself to sleep that night, wondering how I was going to get through the next day. When I woke up, there was no time to think about getting another bottle: I was too involved in looking at the pictures that started to appear before me on the walls of my studio, and then on the wall of the downstairs kitchen where I went to tell the landlady what I was seeing.

Tibor's wife was very sympathetic. She was an English lass a bit older than myself, and having been through the stirrings of the Hungarian revolution on the continent was not disturbed by my condition.

The pictures began as a circle of light dancing on the wall of the studio. As I looked at this light, it changed into the face of an ancient. I thought I was looking at God. It was a very gentle, old, wise face, with white hair, long beard, and antennae coming out of his head. As I was looking at him, he spoke with his eyes, and the face then changed into that of Jesus Christ.

By this time I was on my knees, with tears rolling down my cheeks, saying "I always knew, I always knew". The sense these visions conveyed -- that there was an intelligence within the Universe responsible for its creation -- was too strong to ignore. Through my tears, the pictures kept on coming. Suddenly, to the left of the face of Christ, there began to appear five squares of light similar to television screens.

Each screen contained a different scene. One was of a city full of people running through it, as though they were fleeing from an earthquake. Another was of a different time, with cathedral spires crumbling in the background, as happened during the wars of the middle ages. Another screen depicted a scene of a modern metropolis such as New York City, with people on the streets and automobiles. All the pictures were in black and white, as though they were early video scenes flashing before my eyes. I later learned they were possibly the dreams that had been suppressed during the year of inebriation that Willard had interrupted.

It was my twenty-fourth birthday. My friends had used that as an excuse to have a party, Lena, John, Joan, Pat Webb, Loretta, Willard ... and then, when I protested the attire of a guest they asked Willard to take me home. They were ancient then, and now they're antique. But at that time I probably never would have had such detailed visions if Willard hadn't taken me home early that night.

"Saratoga, 1967: Loretta"

A few days later, it was very calm, quiet, peaceful as I opened my eyes. For a moment I didn't remember where I was. Then I noticed I was naked and didn't remember going to bed. I was in bed, a strange bed, in a room I'd never slept in before. A woman came into the room, sat at the end of the bed, and asked me if she could make love to me. I looked at her in astonishment and said, "I can't imagine why you'd want to!" All I wanted was a drink!

As she moved towards me, pushed aside the sheet and cover and proceeded to kiss my stomach, I felt embarrassed, and knew that I wasn't anything anyone should want to make love to. I began to remember where I was, and then realized that she must have undressed me after I'd passed out on her living room floor. I also realized that she must have put me to bed. I couldn't remember any of it. As she proceeded to kiss me, obviously trying to arouse me, I rose up on one elbow and looked at her. She had her back partially turned toward me. I squirmed away and said, "Where's my bottle?"

She muttered that I'd finished it all the night before, before I'd passed out. I then reached for her, pulled her up to me, looked at her and said,"You put me to bed?"

She said, "Of course, darling. You passed out".

As I tried to pull out of the embrace I was locked into, I announced that I had to visit the powder room. Loretta graciously moved aside; helping me up, she handed me a robe and took me to a little room off the kitchen which had a bathtub, sink and toilet.

While I was showering she asked me if I'd like coffee. I said "not really", and then she brought in towels and a pair of blue pajamas, saying "try these on, I'll fix something!". I turned off the shower and shakily dried my body, put on the pajamas, looked in the mirror and checked out the veins in my cheeks. They were still there. They were the thin red veins usually seen in the faces of heavy drinkers. I'd had them for awhile and had been watching their journey over my face. Thin spider webs of veins, the broken blood vessels of alcoholics.

There were also brown patches at the sides of my

mouth, signs of pellegra, and there were cracks there also, from a thiamine deficiency, I learned later. My gums bled when I tried to brush my teeth, and my hands shook as I tried to light a cigarette. I couldn't eat or drink anything that wasn't alcoholic. The thought of it made me sick to my stomach. Coming out of the porcelain tiled bathroom into the kitchen, I saw the woman who'd put me to bed the previous day, sitting at the plastic-topped kitchen table.

She'd put two glasses of orange juice and cups of coffee at either end of the table. There was an ashtray in the middle, and also an empty chair which was meant for me. I sat down, looked at her defiantly and asked where my bottle was. I was sure that I hadn't finished it as she said I had. She said, "Wouldn't you rather eat something first? Wouldn't you like an egg?"

I said that I couldn't keep anything down, that the thought of it made me sick and that I just wanted a drink. That my hands were shaking, and that I needed a drink to make them stop. I got her to call the liquor store and she managed to have two bottles delivered, a pint of vodka for her and a pint of brandy for me. That's what I asked for. We then sat at the kitchen table, with our glasses and our cigarettes.

When she saw the amount of brandy I poured into the water glass I was using, she looked at me and said soberly, "If you continue to drink like that you'll be dead in ten years". I said, "So what! I never expected to live this long anyway!" At that she poured herself a drink in a water glass as large as mine, and drank it! I saw the color fade out of her face and she suddenly looked very old and feeble. Then we began to talk.

I told her about Sausalito and Sally Stanford's bordello and restaurent and Juanita's restaurent on the ferryboat, and Peggy's Tin Angel, and the Capri on Grant Avenue. She told me that she'd played piano for Billie Holliday during the 1930s and that Lady Day had cued her by saying "Make with the music". She also told me that she was a member of ASCAP. At that time I didn't know what ASCAP was. Loretta told me she'd worked for United Press International for ten years, for the Jungian Institute in New York City for seven years, and that she was now working for the president of a local college.

I told her that I modeled there, in the life art classes, and that Lena had said this was a good way to supplement my income. The girls who were studyng art and who drew me were the same ones that helped out at the Caffe. One of those girls got a MacArthur Grant for her work in New York City years later, and another one married Michael Cooney and they built a house in Connecticut. The girl who got the MacArthur Grant was married to Spalding Gray for awhile. The classes were like slumber parties only I had to hold the pose. Sometimes it was painful; turning into a statue and remaining that way for thirty minutes is hard. It's the art of the "freeze".

So Loretta and I talked the afternoon away. I remember telling her that she reminded me of the "Mad-Woman of Chaillot". After that she called me mad as in crazy, because of the way I drank.

Eventually I lost track of time and Loretta called the rest home she went to to have them come and get her. She left me the keys to the apartment and five dollars for another bottle. As the two old ladies from the rest home came and helped her down the stairs to the car that was waiting out front, she told me I could stay as long as I wanted. But I didn't want to stay there for some reason, and just looked around the place before I left. It was still afternoon, the liquor store was still open. I went to the one on Broadway in Saratoga Springs, got a bottle of French brandy and a bottle of burgundy. Such was my diet at that time. I took both bottles back to my studio and laid down on my brown velvet cover, on the cot facing the window that I looked through to see the leaves and the sky.

Then I looked at the ceiling and saw a Technicolor picture of Loretta in the nursing home, playing cards with a couple of other older people. She was wearing a red and white striped shirt, and looked out at me from the picture above my head as though she knew that I was there and what I was doing. It was as though she was telling the people she was playing cards with what a drunk we had been on, and that she couldn't do those things anymore. She was telling that she'd already been a drunk and was still an alcoholic, and that I'd made her fall off the wagon. She told that I could still drink because I was only twenty-four years old, but that she couldn't anymore and had only fallen off the wagon to help me up onto it. She felt she had to tell me that I'd be dead in a decade if I kept drinking the way I was.

****

"Musings and Conclusion: Saratoga 1967"

****

It's rather obvious why Loretta and I eventually would part company, which we did. After I went to the hospital that her friends ran to see what it was like, I finally returned to California and never saw her again. She died on her birthday, which was on Valentine's Day, in 1981. Loretta was an Aquarian, a translator and a graduate of the Connecticut College for Women. She was a real trouper, as were Lena and Willard.

My foster parents were troupers also ... troupers in the way the word was used in vaudeville. I use the term to describe players or performers that don't get off the stage until the hook comes out to haul them away. For instance, my foster father got reprimanded by the IRS for plying senators with money in exchange for their education votes. It's illegal to bribe U.S. Congressmen. What happened to him was usuual in situations like that, I guess. The IRS fined him an exorbitant amount and he died at the Peninsula Hospital of emphysema in August of 1982. Willard died in August of 1980 and Lena died in December of 1989.

I believe that Death is but a word we say. When people shed their skins, or fly out of their bodies, the spirit becomes part of the universe. I don't know how they manage to get in touch with us again, but they do. I can feel the presence of whatever spirit might be inspiring me for a moment or two. Who knows if the spirit directs us or we conjure up the spirit by thinking about it, or if it's a combination of the two.

Now to return to the summer of 1967, the summer of love. While Loretta was still at the Four Winds home, I had occasion to return to her apartment. Whether it was the next day or the next week I don't recall, but it was sometime before she got out of the hospital. The house on Lake Avenue where Loretta stayed belonged to Dr. Grace Swanner, 107 Lake Avenue in Saratoga Springs. Dr. Swanner's gone now also. She was Loretta's landlady and admired her a lot. Dr. Swanner was a doctor, a gynocologist perhaps, and worked for years at Saratoga Hospital

The thing about Loretta was that she was born in 1901 and was therefore 66 in 1967. She didn't look it! When I saw her I thought she was thirty five or forty. Ironic ... she said that she had thought that I was at least thirty-five because of the way I was acting. I was imitating Peggy Tolk Watkins, the femme fatale of San Francisco's 1950s art world, at the time.

But now this was the spring of 1967, and when I returned to the apartment to take a nap, upon Dr. Swanner's suggestion, I couldn't go to sleep. Instead I spent the time watching dancing characters in the Picasso prints that were hanging on the walls of that second floor room. They were prints from his Rose and Blue Periods, and the event was spectacular.

For instance, I saw the old guitarist of Picasso's Blue Period gently strumming his guitar as he was lounging in the threshold of a doorway. I didn't hear the music. Then I saw the young acrobat at the beach dancing on top of the ball as it rolled gently underneath her delicately prancing feet. It was a gigantic beach ball, resting on the sand in front of a tremendous black man. He must have been a genie at one time.

(Years later I made up a music box tune called "Girl on a Ball" that was played on the piano as part of a larger suite of dances. The whole was called Suite for Picasso. "Girl" was played on the radio in Melbourne, Australia in 1987, twenty years into the future.)

After that vision but still during the same afternoon in the haunted apartment in Saratoga, I saw the Family Saltimbaque on the beach in another print. The father with a big round belly and a funny hat was dancing, as were the children, and next to them the harlequins of the Rose Period were turning cartwhels in the sand. It was as though these scenes were being presented by real actors and actresses on T.V. At this time, in 1967, I hadn't seen television for years. When I had those visions, electrical hallucinations of the stories of history in televised screens as scenes of motion before my eyes, those pictures appeared suddenly, and would probably still be here today if I hadn't discovered how to turn them off.

Were they telepathic transference of some sort or were they all just the contents of my mind suddenly dancing out in front of my eyes? Dr. Swanner was very sympathetic. When I told her I was seeing things she suggested I go upstairs and take a nap, and when I got upstairs, the pictures were dancing.

The apartment had been an alternate studio attached to Yaddo. I've been told that Carson McCullers would be asked to stay there by Elizabethn Ames if she and Katherine Anne Porter were scheduled for a visit at the same time. They didn't get along. I don't know who else might have stayed there over the years. Yaddo would know that. The names, dates, and assigned studios are probably listed in a big leather bound ledger somewhere in the secretary's office.

During that time I was renting my six-room studio for the $10.00 a week that Lena paid me for my duties at the Caffe. Willard had also commissioned a painting from me and set up an account of $100.00 at the delicatessen next door to the Caffe, known as The Executive in those days. He did that to tempt me to eat something other than leftover pastry shells from the Caffe. That was all I was allowed to eat there, as everything else had to be sold. Lena wasn't making any money at the Caffe in 1967; she was just barely breaking even in those days.

I was basically free labor because she'd saved my life by offering me a place to stay, although at the time she didn't know what "dire straits" I was in. The other choice open to me then had been an introduction to a madam in New York City. What saved me from this fate was that, while in Amsterdam, New York before going to Saratoga, I had written my first play, "Sausalito Fairy Tale". With this manuscript in hand, covered with melted wax from candles used to light the room in which I'd worked to write it, I was not just a runaway. I was a writer, deserving of space in the artistic environment of the Caffe Lena.

The fact that Jean Genet had written and paid for the publication of a long poem when he was working at a bookstore on the guays of Paris, in sight of Notre Dame Cathedral, after he'd gotten out of prison illustrated the fact that he was more than just a petty criminal. I think he mentions this in Thief's Journal. Actually, Sartre points it out in his analysis of Genet in Saint Genet. Francois Villon was also saved by creation of the word from hanging. His famous long poem The Great Testament was written so that he might be pardoned during the visit of a prince to his prison. Ironically he was. He was also banished from Paris, and no one knows what became of him except that he did not hang at that time.

Three years after these events and visions of 1967, after my close encounter with the after-effects of alcoholism, I had occasion to visit one of the places that I might have ended up: the miscellaneous ward of a state mental hospital, also a detox ward. Loretta drove me there after beseeching me not to do it. But I couldn't compete with her sanctimonious attitude and didn't know how else to get back to California at that time. I'd met Gail at the Caffe that weekend. She'd been playing for Lena and had impressed me with the strength of her style. She plays blues, and used her body to articulate the emotions of the songs, something not many women seemed capable of doing in those days.

Loretta played the piano, but in 1970 in Connecticut she'd put the piano away in storage and spent her time working in an office in Hartford. She was an editor for a textbook publishing company at that time. One day she informed me of the fact that we had a sado-masochistic relationship. I didn't like that. I didn't approve of it, and used it as an excuse to leave her for the mental hospital.

****
"13 Days In Hell: Norwich, Connecticut, 1970"
****

It was the summer of 1970. Upstate New York was colorful, the trees were in full bloom, the leaves various shades of green. The wildflowers danced in the occasional breeze. I was staying in Saratoga on weekdays, wandering around town in a daze. On weekends I'd go to Connecticut, usually on the bus, sometimes on the train.

One day I woke up in a bed with bars on the window in back of my head. The bed was in a gigantic ward of women in a state mental hospital in Connecticut. It was 6:30 in the morning. Women with short hair in white nurses' dress uniforms were going from bed to bed, waking up the patients, telling them to get in line for their "meds". They'd pull the covers off the patients still in bed after the alarm had rung. The women, tousled and groggy with sleep, clad in short hospital gowns, stumbled, staggered, walked to the line in front of the pharmacy window at the far front end of the ward.

The ward was the home of 80 women. Each one had her own bed. The ward bedroom was divided by a wall that separated the area into two sides. Each side held 40 beds and lodged 40 women. There were isolation cells at the far end of the room. A person would be stripped naked and thrown in the isolation cell for infractions of rules. This was the miscellaneous ward of a gigantic state mental hospital in Connecticut, but I'm sure these wards are to be found in every state mental hospital in every state in America. The history of treatment of the mentally ill has always been horrifying.

Medication was given in the form of a pill and a small paper container of water, and people were watched while they were taking it. After this perverse communion, the patients wandered into the day room, another area as large as the ward room with a nurses' cage to one side. That was where the attendants spent their time, smoking, gossiping, looking at logs and files, talking on the telephone. While the nurses were killing time, entertaining themselves, watching the clock and their unsightly charges, we patients wandered around the room looking for cigarette butts in the ashtrays left over from the night before.

Other attendants from the kitchen had wheeled in breakfast on steel, two-tiered trays with rollers. The patients were told to set up the tables for breakfast, and after this was done everyone was expected to sit down and eat. While everyone else ate the heavy meal of eggs, toast, whatever else was served, I drank coffee. Sometimes I put milk and sugar in it to delay the faintness, the dizzyness experienced from malnutrition.

While they were eating, the other patients struck up friendships with each other and embarked upon relationships, but I didn't want to stay there in that hospital, in that ward. I would excuse myself from the table, taking my coffee to the other end of the room, set up the typewriter and write in a journal. This manuscript turned into a diary of the days spent on the miscellaneous ward. When I finally got out of that place I took it with me, but that was many years ago. The original manuscript is long gone.

While typing in the day room, I was able to retain my identity of artist. But when the clickety-clack of the machine got on the nerves of other patients, I had to stop. Then I would go and participate in the activities of the day -- cleaning the toilets, sweeping and mopping the floors of the shower/bathroom and day room, playing Scrabble with the other patients, or ping pong in the screened-off sun room area. Outside the entrance to the bedroom area of the ward there was a piano, a little upright. Occasionally I would pick out tunes on it from the music book that rested on the ledge above the keyboard.

Many of the women were so stoned from their medication that they were unable or had no inclination to do anything other than sit and smoke, or sit and stare, or wander back and forth, up and down the ward, occasionally trying the locked door. While playing Scrabble with them, I was able to discover that many of my companions were victims of abusive families. One woman said that she went there every year for a "rest". Her husband would bring her in, and then take her home again when her time was up. Sometimes she would stay there for three to six months or longer. It was her country club.

The most tragic patient on our ward was a large woman who wandered around looking for cigarette butts in the ashtrays. One of the permanent patients there told me that this person had been a psychiatrist on the hospital staff at one time, and that she'd flipped and then become a patient. She had a reputation for biting people if angered.

After three days of being observed on the closed,

locked miscellaneous ward, I was allowed to go to the big dining room outside the building, across the ramp that rose above the grounds of lawn, trees and flowers. The dining room was another huge barnlike structure, set up cafeteria-style with trays, silverware and rows and rows of tables and chairs. In one area, off to the side, was a place where the hospital staff ate.
I arrived there, got my coffee, and said hello to the head of the nursing staff (whom I'd met socially before volunteering to be a resident of her establishment), and lingered about the dining area until it was time to go back. At that time the attendant for our section appeared and began rounding up the inhabitants of the miscellaneous ward to be returned for the afternoon medication. The nurse who was sent to get us gestured towards me to return with the group.

To get back to the ward, we had to take the ramp that cut through the grass to the red brick building in which we were confined. The grounds of the hospital were so beautiful, like a park or an estate! And while approaching the ramp, something came over me. I decided to go for a walk on the grass. When the nurse saw me walking away from the ramp, she called my name to come back. As I turned, I saw that all the other patients who'd been in the dining room had also decided to take a walk across the lawn!

I returned to the ramp while the staff ran after the other patients who were taking an after-dinner stroll under the trees, as would be normal activity for people who were visiting a resort. But we weren't guests at a resort or owners of an estate. We were mental patients in a state mental hospital, who had to be rounded up and herded into a locked ward to be given our afternoon medications of Thorazine, Stelazine, Prolyxin, Cogentin, and all the other things, such as shots of the truth serum, Sodium Pentathol.

Sodium Pentathol ... I saw one woman shot up with that. She'd created some sort of a disturbance on the ward, tried to open the windows in the day room and the sun room. The air in the closed miscellaneous ward was stifling. No one seemed to notice it; we were all in such states of trauma, either shock from being in such a place or made groggy and incoherent from the strength of the medication. The nurses surrounded this woman, who called herself Mrs. Wasp; they physically overpowered her, shot her up with something from a hypodermic needle, then strapped her to a bed on the ward and left her.

I looked in on her when I went into the room to get my toothbrush. She was speaking the record of her life. I stood there looking at this woman with short grey hair, who reminded me visually of my foster mother. She was strapped into the bed with a cover over her, babbling into the air, and there was no one listening to her ... no one but myself, in subdued horror. I'd never seen this sort of brutality before. The woman in the bed repeated her name, her birth-place and other information as though she was being questioned. She repeated the same information over and over again.

Perhaps a few hours later, or maybe sometime the next day, they put her in the isolation cell, without any clothes, at the opposite side of the ward. I looked in and saw her wandering around nude in the room. There was a window with bars on it, and she would approach it and look out. When she saw me looking, she asked me to ask the nurse to give her some water. I went and told the nurse that the woman in the isolation cell wanted some water. The nurse said that she would get her some in a little while.

When I went back and told that to Mrs. Wasp, she asked me to get her a knife. I shook my head and moved away from the isolation cell. I wanted to get out of that hospital, and knew that if I brought that woman a knife, I wouldn't be able to get off that floor for a long, long time.

As it happened, I was there in the miscellaneous ward of a state mental hospital in Connecticut for 13 days. It took collect phone calls to my mother in California to negotiate my release. The hospital wouldn't release me unless I had a certain amount of money, enough to pay for a bus trip back to California. My parents sent a money order for $150.00 to the hospital in my name. After a psychiatric evaluation in front of a board of psychiatrists and nurses, I was told that I had five minutes to pack and be ready to go in the car.

I had to remember how to pack, and compose myself for a journey after being locked up in a closed ward for two weeks. Everything was split-second. I had to instantly snap into focus while shaking all over in order to do the transaction at the bank, purchase my ticket to freedom and be on my way. As the armed guards from the hospital put me on the bus to New York City, I wondered what I had done to merit such attention.

The next part of the story explains how the runaway got involved with addiction and substance abuse. What was I doing in San Francisco before I ventured into the Great Northeast on a stolen blue Sunbeam one night?

At that time in the early 1960s, the use of alcohol and controlled substances was considered as behavior enhancements rather then detriments. Self medication wasn't looked at in the same way as it is today. For instance, my foster parents had nightly cocktails of bourbon and water. They had wine with dinner, cock tails after dinner and then Seconal to put them to sleep. Valium was used during the daytime to relieve anxiety, and, of course, smoking. Smoking was a family habit also. In the early 1960s everyone I knew smoked and drank. Everyone except my parents. They couldn't afford it!

****

"Upper Grant Avenue, Beyond and Back: 1964"

****

We were working at the Capri and the Coffee Gallery. The Fox and Hound was just down the way; a Chinese grocery was the usual place to cross over from the infamous corner of Grant and Green in those old North Beach days. Just down the street was the Anxious Asp, where a jazz combo played sultry soul sounds, sending bass notes out into the night, blowing our blues away. As the music swayed the stages of that poetic age, the words of Ginsberg, Rexroth, Ferlinghetti and Kerouac were just beginning to be heard by kids hanging out on the scene.

We were a generation seduced by the muses of dance and poetry: Terpsichore, Euterpe, Melpomene, Thalia, Polyhymnia, Clio, Erato, Calliope, Urania, you were definitely there, on the streets of San Francisco. Across the Bay at the University, a young man named Mario Savio spoke intensely to assembled crowds of the rights of students. There was a manic fanatic looking out through his eyes; I knew he had been heaven-sent ... The future beat playwright Michael McClure was wandering around, looking for something to put him up and bring him down.

I was just trying to survive, working two bars at the same time, making money to stay alive ... that's the way of runaways. Sometimes I danced in nightclubs, made big bucks that way, living in the twilight, never wondering what was to become of me. I was young and pretty then and didn't know about the ways of dives and poverty.

We danced up and down, all around the town, dressing in costumes of purple and black with leather and lace, playing the flute and never thinking of the next day. I was part of the scene of poets, changing the world with screams ... I was a shadow in the background, hanging out with shades in the underground; we were all silhouettes full of dreams...

Talking about the world of Broadway's strip-joint neon glitter nights, the world of Lenny Bruce, and city underworld hypes, the world of single room dwellers and pawnshop sellers, of city missions and one-night flops, the world of Kerouac when he was on a drunk, of Bukowski in L.A.'s skidrow hotel scene, the world of the junkie and the queen ... talking about the city of night, that always swings with a desolate gleam, picked up in graffiti that's on the wall, cryptic messages for the eyes of all, and who will understand the meaning of the scrawl: "Only gutter snipes know the truth of the writing on the wall"?

Who but the anonymous guttersnipe who sees it all?

Hey, Charlie Chaplin, Edith Piaf, Jean Genet, Arthur Rimbaud, Francois Villon, Charles Baudelaire ... all guttersnipes, one and all, at one time or another. Kids on their own, living on the streets, existing on air, like Milarepa when his uncle took his house and threw him out; he had to go up to an empty cave to think over what it was all about.

Milarepa: he starved and thought, materialized a nettle plant, drank leaf tea and grew green hair ... and he wrote songs in his head while starving in the cave in Tibet, far away from anywhere until some hunters came and found him there. They forced him to eat meat that put him back on the wavelength of all those others still down there in the villages below ... people who were living from day to day, working hard to make their pay; they'd spend it on things to make they stay in the lifestyle they thought they'd chosen ... but it was really only karma that kept them chained there in the valley instead of starving in a cave, hallucinating mystically, writing songs telepathically, dreaming constantly.

Ah, to be like Bodhidharma, living in a state of constant rhapsody intoxicated with the ecstasy, found in the starvation of self induced deprivation. He was watching moving pictures on a wall, in a cave without electricity or water, without food or company ... to be able to turn one's mind inside out and see the essence of what it's all about, without losing sanity!

What's all this got to do with North Beach, and the journey down the lost highway? Disorientation of the senses, a lifetime of disciplined destruction, to arrive at the essence of being. It's like chipping away at the mountain to get to the precious vein, mining a shaft for diamonds, dredging the ocean for pearls, searching for the way to turn cinnabar into gold one day...it's a process of elimination for some, this stay on earth today.

What does the body need to stay alive? What does the human being really need in order to survive? Children starving in Africa get a bowl of gruel a day, people starving in North Korea get a bowl of rice a day, people in America, what do we need to survive the same way? Some say $9.00 for food, others need $100.00 for medication; there is no answer, there is no way to gauge what everyone needs to withstand the test of time today ...

****

"1995 Albany Musings: I Should Be Grateful"

****

This cold raw afternoon of November 18, 1995 is spent waking, looking through the closet for a pair of boots to be ready for the snow. Spent the morning making tea, reading paper, reading book, eating toast and potato, taking pills for digestion. Was reading "Hot House" by Jerome Washington, about being in prison. He's written other books, but apparently they're out of print. This writer is black; a picture of his eyes and part of his face are on the cover of this book. He reminds me of my own writing, some of it; he's one of my brothers.

Also feel related to Bernard Berenson, author of "Pretending To Say No" and "User". His stories are of the world of the street addict around Times Square in New York City during the 1970s and '80s. He is also one of my brothers.

The writer's group PEN American Center has just sent me a charity check for $150.00 that I'd applied for to help me pay my medical bills. They are generous; I am foolish, spending more money than I have, getting into debt like the U.S. Government. I should be wiser.

Now upstairs in our house in Albany's South End, using the computer that the guys in prison don't get to use ... I should take advantage of it more often, considering the circumstance of some writers, wandering the streets of the cities, simulating the lauded examples of Jack Kerouac, who scribbled blues down in a 10 cent notebook that he kept in his breast pocket. I am lucky to be able to use this computer, therefore I should do it.

Reality therapy: I should write about the reality of waking up in our old apartment on Eagle Street across from the Governor's Mansion in Albany, with pots on the floor to catch the water as it dripped from the ceiling, falling down overhead ... similar to the lobby of the Anglo Hotel on Sixth Street in San Francisco that had pots in the lobby to catch the rainwater. That was a shocking place, finally destroyed by the earthquake of 1989. Only shocked victims of Thorazine and lobotomy could live there oblivious to the obvious abandonment. Only alcoholics existing in the other dimension of hallucination could stand to continue to pay rent there.

The rugs on the floors in the room still held the stories of the travelers who'd walked on them and left their stains of pain, tears, urine, wine, beer, coffee, tea, soda, cigarettes, pot, speed, heroin, cocaine ... the rugs had never been cleaned. The beds were the same. The person I'd visited the Anglo with was so down at the time that she acted as though it was a death sentence to have to rent a room there.

Years later, after she'd tried to kill me, I heard from her on a postcard that she was living there. Then the earthquake came and it was destroyed. I read in the San Francisco "Street Sheet" several years later that the occupants who'd been there at the time of the earthquake were eligible for reimbursement checks for the rooms they'd lost to the disaster

Sixth Street in the morning: a desolate place. The street sweepers hardly ever roll along San Francisco's Sixth Street. There are bodies lying in doorways there, at least there used to be. I once saw a Hindu landlord scream at a passed-out woman that she couldn't crash in his doorway. Customers wouldn't want to stay in a hotel that had a woman passed out on its welcome mat! She was too out of it to understand what he was yelling about. I also saw a Chinese grocer there leap over his counter and kick a black man in the chest for stealing a plum. The plum only cost a few cents, and the grocer could have afforded to give it to the thief but he'd rather hit him instead.

In the background, the notes of a sad clarinet sound

from the tape recording of a piece I made to remind me of the foghorns on the bay in the early morning city.

The check from PEN was as a jump-start to a car. I'd sent them a copy of my book, Street Kids and Other Plays, along with the application for emergency assistance and my dentist bills, to show them my progress and my need.

Currently we're living in Albany's South End. I call it Bronzeville. The Governor doesn't live anywhere nearby, but the roof is whole and the inside of the house is dry, as it should be. We're going to have a book-signing party for "Street Kids" in January. I've been inviting people to each read a scene from the book that night. In exchange they'd be treated to a meal, because performers are paid in meal at Mother Earth's where the event will be held.

I also have to start a paper for the class in substance abuse that I'm taking as part of the Master's program at Russell Sage. I started going to school there in 1990, five years ago. I got my Bachelor's degree in Sociology in 1995, and am now working on my Master's in Community Psychology, a new area, an activist's discipline to create positive change in existing social agencies and as a preventive measure to curtail problems in the community; hopefully it will be a way to combat the prejudice and violence associated with it.

Is there a story here? Would some call it quits? What are the reasons behind addiction, what causes addiction to an illegal substance? Circumstances and prior knowledge have a lot to do with it. Ah, well ... must make a new bibliography for the latest paper now, and read, read, read, as we say.

****

"San Francisco: Summer of 1980"

****

It was an experiment. We slept outside, in a doorway, on a rooftop, for a couple of days. I was working as a clerk-typist for the Federal Office of Civil Rights, and my partner was living on a small disability check. She wanted me to feel the plight of the homeless, didn't think the Government understood and thought that if someone attached to it could be made to feel the pain, then attitudes would change.

Next day at the office I felt so exhausted, wearing the same clothes that I'd worn to work the day before ... I had to keep kicking myself to stay awake. I felt dirty, wrinkled, disempowered and poverty stricken. I'd sunk to the depths of the clientele of the Social Security Department's SSI population. It didn't take long to feel that bad. What was it like to feel that way for a lifetime?

On that first day, we woke up in the doorway of the San Francisco Art Institute, at the bottom of Chestnut Street along a boulevard that goes over the Golden Gate Bridge. First thing, we tried to panhandle change for coffee, and suddenly I was in the position of the vets who used to strip me of my change every morning on my usual 12-block walk to work.

From the Harbor Hotel on the Embarcadero to the Federal Building on 13th Street, I'd be accosted by guys who'd smoked or drank themselves to sleep in the doorways of Market Street the night before. They watched me as frequently as I looked at them, every weekday morning, about seven a.m., after emerging from the hotel in my jeans and tennis shoes. Invariably men -- as many as four of them -- would surround me saying "Give us some money for coffee ... come on ..." They scared me. After surrendering the two dollars I had, I'd have to borrow another two dollars at work for my own needs, but then I was able to get it there and they weren't.

They'd fought in Vietnam, and who knows what had happened to them over there. It's terrible to be in the same clothes for twenty-four hours, let alone forty-eight or seventy-two ... unless one is starving, in the throes of alcoholism or on dope of some sort ... heroin, meth, alcohol, LSD ... or on a three-day bus trip and doesn't feel the discomfort of old dirt and clothes.

****

"The Orange Nightmare": Aftermath

****

On the three-day bus trip from Connecticut to California, I spent the time looking out the window drinking in the scenes of America as they flashed by and learning how to sit in the seat and act like a "lady" by watching the other women on the bus. Pretending I hadn't been where I'd been! Trying to forget it, and now, 25 years later, writing about it upon the suggestion of a friend.

When I had to change buses at the Port Authority in New York City, I realized that my conditioning had been broken. Being locked up and treated like a criminal for thirteen days on a ward with women who had been there for decades had been deadly to my fragile sanity.

The coffee that I'd been living on there had, without my knowledge, been laced with medication which also caused me to forget how to act like a lady out in public. Under its influence, I'd been locked up for thirteen days with only the other patients and a view from the hospital windows as intellectual stimulation.

I'd been put on the bus in Connecticut by armed guards after being driven away from the hospital in a black limousine. My mind had been emptied, wiped out! I rode into the Port Authority and then had to change buses, suddenly having to function as a capable human being after being treated like a non-person. As I carried my suitcase and typewriter off the incoming bus and found the bus to California, I was shaking.

I took a seat near the window, and as we were pulling out of the station a copy of the latest Esquire Magazine caught my eye. On the cover was a picture of Dustin Hoffman, set against the city skyline. The caption read, "Dustin Hoffman Grows Up." I thought that was ironic, as the script that I'd been writing at the MacDowell Colony earlier that year was called "War Baby Grows Up"! It had been read by an agent from the William Morris Agency and tabled for being "ten years ahead of its time"; yet a tiny thread of the same reality had made it to the newsstands! Such were my thoughts as the Greyhound bus pulled out of New York City.

Traveling across the country without a radio or anyone to talk to, I remembered the poor people still locked up in that concentration camp I'd just escaped from. I slept, ate Lifesavers, drank coffee and soda at the rest stops, and looked out the window as the days and nights passed.

When we rolled into the L.A. station there was a three-hour wait for the bus to northern California. I put a quarter in the tiny TV in the bus station and lost myself in the ballet that was performing Stravinsky's Firebird Suite in contemporary mode. It was a Balanchine rendition. The ballerinas were in slips dancing about on what appeared to be a rooftop. I realized that the ballerina portraying Firebird was being played as if she were mad. The dancer reminded me of myself in a slip in wilder years, or one of those sad women I'd left behind on the ward.

In retrospect, from a distance of 25 years, I realize now that it might have been the choreographer's interpretation of the sadness of the beats as reflected in the madness of the hippies of the 1960s. The soul of our ideas would rise from the ashes of our sacrificed lives and minds. Our ideas would survive. Flower power, peace, love, brotherhood ... along with some of us.

Then it was time to get back on the bus again. Settling in, I looked out the window and noticed the name of a performer up in lights on one of the theaters in the Sunset Strip, which we were passing on the way out of town. The name I saw was Don McLean. This brought back memories, of me plucking the strings of his guitar at Lena's house in Saratoga before one of his performances there, and talking to an editor of prison poetry who was in residence at Yaddo. We spoke of the conscientious objectors who'd taken refuge in Canada until the general amnesty was declared.

After that late-night conversation one Saturday, I'd wandered up to the Caffe and Lena asked me if I would read a poem to the audience during a break in the folk-singer's set. I just happened to have one in a pocket that I'd been working on. It was addressing America's position in the world. After my reading the audience clapped and I retreated from the stage. I left the Caffe and went around the corner to Caroline Street to sit in and sing a song with Bob Warren's band.

Remembering, riding on the bus, trying to recall the rest of my identity, I focused on my unmade movie script, "War Baby Grows Up", also called "Shadows From A Shattered Prism". One sing-song phrase from that script kept running through my mind like a children's street song:

"Hiroshima, Nagasaki, 1945,
God sighed, the world cried,
children pursued suicide..."

Children pursued suicide. That phrase encapsulated the reason behind the insanity of the hippies of the 1960s. Somehow our taking of LSD, methamphetamines and heroin was connected to the existence of the bomb, and the fact of the terrible future atomic explosions.

We didn't know the drugs would hurt us. We wanted to feel good ... everyone else was doing it. We were young and didn't know how fragile our minds and bodies were, that it didn't take an atomic bomb to destroy the delicate chemical balance of our physiology.

"We flew into the sun,

we transcended time,
becoming ghostly
    people ...
poets thought death
our only design."

We got hepatitis and malnutrition, we went crazy in the streets. Throwing away our white middle-class heritage, we were opening the door for the third world kids who'd never had the advantages of growing up in automatized, movie-oriented suburbia. We became heroin addicts, happily wandering the streets, looking for the dealer to come down like an angel from the sky to keep us high ... and then the bubble burst and we all came down like Humpty Dumpty, crashing to the ground.

Now in the last decade of the 20th Century there are thousands, if not millions of homeless, disoriented people wandering the streets of the cities of America and Europe. How many of these people were once beatniks? How many were once hippies? How many are veterans of World War Two, the Korean Conflict or the Vietnam Era?

While on the bus in 1970, riding back to California, I remembered a phrase that had come into my head while locked up on the miscellaneous ward: "Everyone who passed through the 1960s is sick and has to be recycled ... " As I look upon this phrase again I remember the 1970s and the SLA, a movement that promoted a return to the values of the 1950s.

Disguised as a revolutionary act of terrorism at its onset, when the kidnapping and subsequent bent-mind drug trip of third world sex and revolution was finally played through, what emerged was a return to the forgotten 1950s middle class lifestyle of love and marriage, little diamond rings and parenthood.

But all that was a part of the future, unknown to me on that day riding the Greyhound bus back to California from my two week vacation in the hospital back east. The bus swept out of Los Angeles into the desert of an Indian reservation, vast expanses of dry tumbleweed and cactus-covered acres. I managed to collect my wits and make a phone call at the next rest area and arranged to stop off in San Mateo to visit my foster parents before traveling on to Chico to see my mother. In San Mateo I stayed overnight at the Saint Matthew's Hotel, and had coffee with my foster mother the next day.

Wanting to alert me to the state of the revolution since I'd been away, she looked at me with her steel-grey eyes and said that the Indians had reclaimed Alcatraz. I didn't understand the significance of that heroic act, and just thought it was great that they had decided to camp out there.

After this indecisive brunch, I got back on the bus and traveled through San Francisco, past Sacramento to Chico, to my mother, brothers and sisters ... people I hadn't seen since the early '60s when I'd run away. I'd been gone since 1961. Now, eight years later, I showed up, a fugitive from a nuthouse, disoriented, without money, clothes, job or home. It's taken me years to recover from those thirteen days spent in that Godforsaken place full of lost souls, caught as in scenes from Dante's Inferno.

Of course before I went there I painted Fragments of Light. Talking about thirteen actual paintings done in

Saratoga Springs from 1965-1967:

****
"Fragments of Light"
****

Charlie Chaplin and the Crow, somewhere in Canada, painted in Saratoga, 1966 ... and the portrait of Mississippi John Hurt on a dancing chair, given to Hattie's for safekeeping one year, got stolen they say ... and so did the others, thirteen paintings, created while the music of Pat Webb played in the background, and snow covered the ground ...

There was a picture of a blue rat leaping over a red brick wall, and the portrait of three pink pigs in a field, doing a jelly roll ... there was one pig that went to Canada as a gift to a friend, and a picture of a Tiger on a field of golden grain ... there was a round picture of a psychedelic clown, dancing in a spiderweb with a chessboard background, looking like Prince Valient in a blue dungaree suit ... it was a gold and silver spiderweb on a round background ...

There was a Jack-in-the-Box in a toy room, and War Baby on the road, surrounded by buildings tumbling down,all around, surrounded by ruins of the city on the ground ... Tambourine Man danced on the rainbow sands, waving his instrument in his hand ... his words used to live in my head until I replaced them with words of my own, taken from things that I've said and done ... remembering all those pictures, and wondering whatever became of them ... are they gathering dust, day after day? Hey, Mr. Tambourine Man, where you gonna play now, what you gonna say?

There was a picture of three newsboy street kids sleeping together against a blue stone wall. I'd made it with acrylics and oils, from a subject in a picture of old New York. I gave it to Loretta in 1967 and haven't seen it since. She wouldn't tell me what she did with it. Once she said she left it in the closet at 107 Lake Avenue in Saratoga. I asked Dr. Swanner before she died and she said that she didn't remember seeing it.

Loretta lied all the time. Her real name was Mary. She'd translated a life of Michaelangelo from or into the Italian. I didn't know that till I'd looked her up in the Library of Congress on-line listings, along with myself.

End Part Two

****
****

PART THREE:

WASHED BY THE RAIN

PART III

WASHED BY THE RAIN

Tim Burgess 98

Preface: "The Typist"

(Written for Jack Kerouac, after the 1996 New York University "Beat Generation" Conference

Truman Capote called him a typist.
His writing was straight narrative, prose without
a break for punctuation, like
a car speeding along a highway
in the night, no need to stop for crosswalks,
intersections, headlights ...

a car "On the Road",
racing into the midnight
with wild angels for company ...

... Neal Cassady did the driving, Jack the riding,
in a stolen car sometimes ... racing with the dawn
of a crimson sun rising ahead in the
far distant future of a new morning ...

creating "The Golden Eternity"
of this resurrection we are feeling,
that the audience is experiencing.

The reasons for not publishing the novel that he'd
worked on for seven years were petty ...
the houses didn't think that they'd make money,
like the merchants in the temples of
the ancient days ...

the palaces of publishers are cautious when it
comes to unknown producers of untested products,

unknown writers of unread books ...
items presented in cardboard boxes,
with unconventional, non-academic style.

Of course that attitude changed as soon as
his friend screamed with a cry that sobbed
the desperation of the desolation of
the "best minds" of their generation ...
the "best minds" of their generation ...
Allan Ginsberg in 1956 at the 6 Gallery.

The HOWL was heard, promoted by the cheering
of the "typist", who worked the crowd for change,
for wine to keep the feeling flowing, while
the tears were spilling as the rage was growing,
tumbling in cascade through cadences of
injustice and accusation ...

The silence was broken, as spectacular reaction
to oppression initiating the call to action, and
the Angel of Apocalypse played his horn
in mime of the trembling times ... while "Strange
Fruit" was still swaying in the Southern breeze.

Talking 1956, in the City by the Bay, with
jazz on the Embarcedero, Charlie Parker blowing "Now's
The Time", Billie Holliday singing "God Bless
the Child", as Louis and Duke played strong on the
other side of town, in the background ...

Odetta was banging out folk on a magic guitar,
Bobby Dylan was in high school, absorbing it all,

talking San Francisco in the fifties was
the place to be.

The "typist" was there, travelling around,
recording pictures of the underground, collecting
notes for later narrations, creating
portraits for transcription ...

The "typist" was perhaps a reincarnation
of Jack London, perhaps it's true ...

****
"Subterranean Love in the Shadows: 1971"
(an animation for shadows and shades)
****

Set: A crowded theater. The character on the stage, standing at the podium, is clad in black, a ninja costume, with a white mime face. Members of the audience are also in black with white mime faces, but the expressions painted on them are of other races. The costumes consist of T-shirts and tights for females, T-shirts and sweat pants for males, projecting the aura of chicks and cats, a very "hip to the vernacular" scene.

On one side of the theater, a chick in a long black lace dress, tights and mime face is lounging on a ledge. She's looking at the stage and then at the mezzanine, worriedly searching the boxes above the area. Suddenly, from the middle of the audience, a cat rises, a male in black sweat pants and black striped T-shirt, with a black kerchief around his neck, conveying the impression of a French apache.

He crosses to the ledge and stealthily leaps up, settles down next to the chick. He edges over to her. Startled, she turns to look at him. Then he says something soothingly, to arrest her apprehension.

CAT: Oh, it's you!

Just then, the audience bursts into applause, and the cat on the stage dances around and then jumps down, as another takes his place, and begins to read from a bundle of papers that he shuffles around on the podium. The cat on the ledge nudges closer to the chick, till their shoulders are touching, and again the audience erupts into applause, as the cat on the stage is replaced by another ...

The lighting changes gradually to black, and then comes up again, this time on a park bench. To one side, as a backdrop, is a church; across the stage, on another backdrop, is a theater. The bench is in the middle of a park; there are shrubs and trees on the backdrops between the church and the theater. Two silhouettes on the park bench are curled into each other, as in a lovers' embrace.

The moment is broken as we hear the explosion of a gun going off in the distance. The chick rises hurriedly and runs offstage, as the cat is left on the bench, alone, and the lights fade to black.

****

"Stuff"

(for Mother)

****

The set: We see one of those rambling two-story farmhouses, with a big front porch, on a half acre of land, and there are sheds in the back. It is midnight, all the lights in the house are on. A figure can be seen working, going from the first floor to the second floor, carrying bags and boxes of clothing, papers, toys ... the bags and boxes have names written on them with a black felt pen ... Andy, Kathy, Christopher, Jimmy, Tony, Philip, Peter, Veronica, Mari-Beth, Sylvia, Brio ...

There is no front on this two-story set, so we are able to see the Actress, climbing the stairs from the first to the second floor and going through the rooms, sorting the stuff. She's talking to herself while doing this, a steady stream of monologue. Every once in awhile we hear a dog bark ... and the howling of the wind outside as it rustles the leaves on the trees.

The Actress is a middle aged woman with glasses. She has frizzy, short hair and an air of madness, which she carries around like a hard-earned cloak or laurel wreath of fame. She looks like a healthy version of Marcel Marceau's interpretation of the overcoat clerk in his play of the same name ... an exhausted woman, who could play Medea.

As the lights come up, she is heard mumbling to herself as she climbs the inside staircase to the second floor. She's carrying a box with the name "PHILIP" on it; we begin to hear her voice distinctly:

ACTION

ACTRESS: Where am I going to put all this stuff? It's suffocating me. He doesn't care ... he's down there in his house with his paints, and his tools, and his pension, and his money ... being just as selfish as he's always been!

She reaches the top of the stairs, puts the box down and goes into the middle room. The name "SYLVIA" is written above the door. Inside there's a canopied double bed decorated with pink lace and a white spread. At the foot of the bed is a trunk and a chest of drawers. Stacked up along the walls there are more boxes, with the names on them again ... JIMMY, CHRISTOPHER, ANDY, KATHY, BRIO, MARI-BETH, PHILIP, PETER, VERNICA, SYLVIA, TONY ...

ACTRESS: And his kids are the same as he is, just a pack of no-good bums ... leaving all this stuff here for me to sort and store. Their clothes, their books, their toys ... this is MY house. My father bought it for me. But how can I live this way with all their things taking up space? It's as though I've been cursed,that old Scottish curse left over from Robert the Bruce and Pope Innocent the Third. It's driven me crazy all my life!

(The sound of wind chimes coming from below causes her to turn and go back down the stairs to see who it is she has to see now. We hear her say ...)

Oh, Philip! What are you doing today? We have a lot to do if you're here to stay!

(The lights dim as the set fades to black.)

****

"Prelude to 'Reality #1': Winter 1994"

****

Hurrying back from lunch along the busy winter sun-drenched street, to the side of me there's a person crawling to his feet. Out of the gutter he steps; holding onto the street lamp post for support, he says, "Hey, Miss". I turn to look at him, side-ways. While hanging onto the lamppost, he edges closer to me so that I can see how many times his nose has been broken.

He says, "I ain't retarded ... I just need some change so I can get a drink. I won't lie to you about it! I just need a drink ... "

I look at him, reach my hand in my pocket, feel some coins, pull them out, two dimes and a penny, give them to him and then continue on my way back to the office. I cross the street as the light changes, go up the cobblestone passageway that sometimes reminds me of Lombard Street in San Francisco. Walk past the Omni Hotel into the office building, carrying my package of Christmas presents bought on the lunch hour. I get to my desk, put down the packages, take off my coat, turn on the radio and begin to type. Remembering that night long ago in Saratoga at the Caffe Lena, when I once asked someone for a dollar for a drink!

That was in 1967, some thirty years ago ... she gave me the dollar, and I went back into the kitchen and gave it to John, my partner in crime at the time. He went off and got a bottle of whatever it was that we were drinking. We were always drinking then; it was cheaper than food. The woman who gave me the dollar for the drink that day eventually drove me out of town and into a new life, one without the bottle, without John and the Caffe ... and the door closes on the world of yesterday as reality rushes in on another first day of winter at the office ...

****

"Reality #1"

****

He wore a cap that said "Cat"; he was
tall and lean, like an Abe Lincoln scene,
said he needed a paper from the Welfare to
admit him to a shelter; he could hardly
say the words as a worker appeared,
said that she'd help him,
but to sit on the bench
till she'd found his rent.

Then he started punching at the air,
saying things 'bout the life out there.
The brutality of his mimed scream
was easily seen by the gestures
enacted as he told his dream.

In pantomime he danced a rhyme,
of fighting, hitting, killing, dying ...
mumbling screams, a hand-jive kata
that told a story that we all know
from TV street-war scenes.

The worker returned with the uniformed guards
to escort this cat to where
they'd filled out the form of a habitat ...
it happened just like that.

He was wasted and beat, seeking
shelter from the heat, like a
runaway coming in from the street.

He could have been Christ, this man with no wife
to comfort his tears when he's feeling forlorn ...

Downcast, torn apart by life's blast,
just another one of those expensive winos
coming home at last, carrying DTs around
like a sack from the past ...

All those pictures in his head, nowhere to put them,
enough said.

****

"Marilyn: 'Death Is But A Word We Say'"

****

The woman bore a striking resemblance to Marilyn Monroe, the icon of American Feminine Sexuality during the 1950s. Could it be that perhaps Marilyn didn't die, but instead, that night in the Hollywood hospital, was punched in the chest, told to throw up all the alcohol and pills she'd swallowed, and then whisked away to a private mental hospital? Perhaps this is her story.

Since her funds were considerable, she was able to pay for personal attention. Time passed, and with it, the electroshock treatments she'd been given in 1962 were replaced by the drugs that render longterm, rather than instant, dementia. Years continued to float away, and as administrations changed, presidents died and were replaced, and Hollywood itself was rearranged, the star that Marilyn had been was no longer. Her mind and body were gone.

Studios only in business for the money had replaced the focus on people that the old star system had generated for years. The organizations that took over made movies from formulas guaranteed to double and triple the original cost invested in productions. The formulas were determined by polls and audience surveys that gauged which movies made the most money and had the greatest audience turnover.

An analysis of the content of these films found them to be composed of the tension of violent sexual hysteria married to the panic of terror. These new movies recreated the excitement of war on the screen, whether it was in the streets, the home or the corporation conference room. The innocent situation comedies that Marilyn had made were now to be found in prototype as soap operas watched daily by America's housewives.

The market had changed, Hollywood had changed, the star system had been dominated by musicians since the 1960s. The poetic British skinny boys had been on the stages of America since early in the decade. Their made up, clean exteriors had cut into the American entertainment market in a big way. Hardly anyone went to movies in the '60s; the kids were watching the pictures they saw in their heads when they took pills.

Marilyn knew about moving pictures and pills. They gave her pills at the hospital, the many hospitals she'd been in and out of for thirty years, ever since that night she died. The studio had staged a funeral complete with body. One of her many body doubles had OD'd that night. No one had been able to tell the difference between the two of them in life, much less in death, so the real Marilyn was able to be sedated and established in a private sanitarium for addicts with no one the wiser.

This new person, after spending thirty years in rest homes and state institutions, was finally deemed fit to be released onto the streets of the country. She was thiry years older and thirty pounds heavier. She hadn't really aged, other then gaining weight. Even though her hair was a different color, and the protection of the Studio was no longer there, the resemblance to her younger self was undeniable. Her voice was the same; only the dialogue was different.

Norma Jean Baker had been experiencing the world of her mother for the last thirty years. After her suicide attempt and removal to a private hospital for diagnosis and subsequent longterm therapy, she was declared disabled and thereby entitled to all the benefits that such status entails. She was released to a halfway house, a group home for the mentally disabled. There were rules, as in any group home. Residents were to be in at certain hours, up and dressed in time for medication and breakfast, and they were given until three weeks after their arrival to find a hotel room in the regular community.

Norma Jean found things to be quite different at this level of society than she had ever known them to be. Even though she was thirty years older and thousands of miles away from L.A., she was still as a child when it came to dealing with people. She held her age well despite the extra weight, dyed hair and lack of money. Her voice hadn't changed ... it was undeniably the child-voiced Marilyn Monroe. It was hard to believe. Of course most people didn't notice the similarity, and even fewer recognised the voice, though they did think it familiar.

While in the group home, with the aid of another released patient, Norma Jean did manage to find a room in one of the transient hotels on the poorer side of town. In the hotel, she tried to sleep until her next disability check came, but kept waking up with horrible headaches. She'd take herself to the hospital, present her Medicaid card and ask for help to take away the pain. Eventually, after she started to scream, a staff member on duty would give her something to quiet her down, but it never helped: a combination of Empirin and codeine that only made her wish for ice cream. She hated these pills, and wished that she would meet a doctor who'd give her the medication she needed to make the pain go away once and for all.

Her mother had suffered the same kind of intolerable pain, as had her grandmother. Her mother had finally been given a lobotomy in the hospital. The operation had reduced her to a docile, willing patient, eager to please. Gone was the fiery personality of the hard-working woman with a daughter to care for. Marilyn's soul cried for her mother, but there was nothing she could do for her, other than try to make as much money as possible to share with her.

When her mother eventually died from old age, cancer and the side-effects of psychotropic medications, Marilyn was well into her career. When Norma Jean heard that her mother had passed away in her sleep one night, on the ward that she hadn't wanted to leave since her operation, Marilyn wept and sent flowers. Of course there was a funeral, and the Star was there with members of her entourage and some of the attendants from the hospital, and when it was over, Norma Jean Baker, a.k.a. Marilyn Monroe, was left alone with her memories, and finally, the rest of her life.

****

"Looking For A Room: San Francisco 1978"

(a modern-day gothic story)

****

Ruby, a woman in her late 30s, wandered through the rain falling down on the late night North Beach night-club scene. Her whole world was suddenly collapsing around her, it seemed. The bar she hung out in was going to be sold. She'd finally been rousted by the police from the condemned building she'd appropriated as a studio when she was a student at the San Francisco Art Institute. Ever since Chin Wah Lee had died, things had been going badly for her.

The girl she'd been running with for the past year had become incredibly sadistic and selfish. She'd been doing nothing but snorting and shooting coke, conning her father's business managers for more money from her trust fund, then buying expensive sports cars and wrecking them one right after another. She liked to speed through the night stoned on a combination of LSD, hashish, cocaine and liquor, constantly smoking pot with all these things swirling around in her brain.

It was becoming obvious that Pat was going slightly insane.

Ruby thought about her friend's suicidal lifestyle as she was going from Hotel to hotel, trying to find a room to rent for the night. She was tired and hungry. The life she'd been leading was so exhausting. She was never able to sleep anymore, even when she had a place to crash. It had been nice when the bar was open. That had been a fun place to go. Perhaps if she'd appreciated it more at the time it would still be open today, instead of her having to move to the other side of town, so far away.

"Hey, babe, you got a cigarette?"

Ruby stared at the voice coming from the ragged figure standing in the doorway of the hotel where she'd just asked for a room. The kid wasn't very impressive, torn tennis shoes, torn gray sweatshirt, torn corduroy pants. In fact, everything about him seemed to be in tatters. There was a bandage on his nose and a cast on one of his arms, with words written all over it. He was leaning on a pair of crutches with a grin on his face.

"Sure, pal, take this one. It's all I got at the moment ... ".

Ruby extended the cigarette she'd been smoking to the kid with the crutches, and suddenly felt better. Sure, she had scars on her wrists from the razor blades, but at least she didn't have to have crutches and a cast. "Say, do you know where I can rent a room for awhile? Just me and my dog?"

The kid took a drag from the cigarette. "Maybe ...

let's go for a walk. There's a guy I know, owns a hotel down on the waterfront. He usually has vacancies."

The Harbor Hotel, on the San Francisco Embarcadero next door to Earthquake McGoon's Dixieland jazz music place, was a famous old hotel. Its interior had been used in movies set in San Francisco's bootleg era of the 1920s and '30s, but Ruby didn't know this yet. All she knew, after her walk through the city from North Beach to the Embarcadero, was a dingy glass-paned door that opened into a lobby with a front desk and a clerk. There was a promising sign on the wire cage behind which the clerk sat. The sign said VACANCY.

When Ruby saw this, she began to beam from head to toe, while saying in a childlike voice, "I'd like to rent a room please, what are your rates?"

The clerk looked at the urchin, and then looked in a receipt book. "$20.00 a week without bath", he said, "bathroom's down the hall, shower's down the hall too. $20.00 a week in advance! How many pets you got?"

"Just one" answered Ruby, who was looking at the people sitting in the lobby and noticing that they all looked as tattered and torn as the fellow who'd brought her to the Harbor. When she looked back at the clerk, she said, "Could I please see the room first?"

"Sure ... George", he called to one of the people sitting in the lobby, "take these keys, 314, 213 and 416, and show the little lady the rooms, please."

"Okay", came from the mouth of a slender, humpbacked older man in his 60s who walked with a cane. "Let's ride the elevator. It's faster and easier."

"Okay", said Ruby, and the two moved a few steps to the other side of the lobby, where the elevator could be heard churning behind antique metal doors with glass windows. After a few moments there was a thud. The elevator had landed.

The doors rolled open and a couple of younger people emerged from its beige interior. They nodded to George, who held the keys to the empty rooms, and looked with curiosity at the new tenant. Ruby and George entered the box and rode to the second floor. Upon emerging, Ruby noticed the torn green carpet on the floor, and the winding corridor with numbered doors on either side of the hallway. There was an aura of unquestionable mystery, of tawdry, bawdy San Francisco history about the place.

The room, 213, had a brass bed, a large wooden bureau with a mirror, and a window that looked out into a parking lot. From there one could see the freeway that ran above the Embarcadero Highway, and the sidewalk that ran alongside the old railroad tracks below it. There was a tattered lace curtain hanging over the window, with a Venetian blind that was yellowed by time. In a corner of the room was a sink. The bed was next to a closet in the middle of the space. Next to that was a night table with a ceramic lamp and an armchair.

"Where's the bathroom?" Ruby asked the man who was showing the room.

"Down the hall, around the corner. There's one on every floor. They've got showers on every floor also. So how you like the room?"

Ruby looked at the furniture. 'It'll do', she thought, and then walked towards the window and looked out. "Some view ... " she said, grinning back at George, who was waiting for her answer. Ruby decided that she'd look at the rest of the vacancies; after all, she was going to have to live in the dump. But then, it had been such a long time since she'd even been allowed to look at rooms that this kind of choosing was like an adventure, like a treasure hunt of "looking for a room".

She looked at George and said matter-of-factly, "Could I see the other vacancies before I decide?"

George said, "Sure. Come this way." and with a flourishingly antique bow, as if he was a courtier from another country, another time, he ushered the woman out the door. "We could take the stairs to the next floor," he said. "That way you'll know where they are, in case you decide to stay with us for awhile."

"Yeah", said Ruby, "I like exercise ... been getting a lot of it these past few months." George looked at her appraisingly. "Yeah, you look pretty fit, for someone in their thirties. After all, that's almost middle-aged, isn't it?" Ruby was crestfallen at this slur towards her fleeting youth. "Yeah, like the 1960s was a very exhausting time. It was like living on a roller coaster in a carnival. We were living in a party all the time ... weren't you in the City then?"

George suddenly felt a little embarrassed. As a bit of a blush crept across his decadent features, he struggled to change the subject. "Uh, here's number 314". He inserted the key into the lock and the brown wooden door swung open.

The inside back wall was a set of two windows, with a fire escape landing outside. The bed, placed in front of the windows, took up one-third of the space because it was a double. At the front of the bed was a brown bureau with a mirror attached to it. The steel frame of the bed fit snugly into the space between the front of the bureau and the wall on the opposite side of the room.

Standing against the wall down from the bureau was a refrigerator. Next to that was a small table. On it was a two-burner hotplate next to a small cabinet in which silverware, dishes and other articles were kept. There was a sink next to an antique wardrobe that served as a closet, which stood near the door. On the wall opposite the door was a picture in a frame of some flowers, and below that an incongruous armchair. A floor lamp with an old-fashioned cloth lampshade was a finishing touch, which helped make the room appears more comfortable than one might have expected.

Ruby suddenly felt tired, as though she'd reached the end of a long journey and had finally found a place to rest. She sat down on the bed with an air of weariness and looked out the window at the freeway and the cars racing by overhead. The faint sound of music drifted up from the jukebox in the bar next door to the hotel. Someone had played a song that was one of Ruby's favorites. As she sat upon the bed, she sang one of the refrains and decided that she liked this place.

"Okay, I'll take this one. How much is it?"

"$20.00 a week."

"Where do I pay?"

"Downstairs at the front desk."

"Okay, let's go."

George opened the door, and after he went out Ruby stayed for a moment in this space. She felt tears well up in her eyes while she was turning herself away from the little view of the freeway and the bay. She went out the door and, while walking behind George along the corridor, started going through her pockets to make sure she had enough money for the first week's rent. Remembering she'd put her bills in her shoe, and seeing that George was turning the corner to the staircase, she bent down to quickly extract three bills, two for the rent and the third to use as pocket money on the streets. Arriving at the desk, Ruby saw that the clerk was listening to George telling him that the new tenant was about to pay her first week's rent on that old vacant room on the third floor, number 314.

Both men looked up as Ruby approached the desk, with the money in her hand so that they'd know she was serious about the business transaction. "I'd like to rent number 314", she said.

The clerk reached under the counter for the receipt book and replied, "You want it by the week? By the month?"

"I'll start off by the week, and then if I like it, I might pay by the month."

"Okay, little lady, let's make out the receipt. You just sign on the dotted line, and everything will be fine!".

Turning to Ruby, George asked, "You sure you like the room, Miss?"

Ruby, looking from George to the clerk behind the cage, replied, "Yeah, it's got a nice view, and I like the fire escape being there, never can be too safe ... I think I'll be just fine. I can hear the music from the jukebox in the bar next door. Oh, is it okay for me to have my dog here? She's a German shepherd mix named Ivy, and she doesn't bother anyone. She's housebroken ... "

The two men looked at each other again. Finally the clerk said, "Oh, yeah, sure! Here now, you just sign on the dotted line and your rent will be paid for a week!" Again Ruby felt the tears well up in her eyes as she signed the receipt and gave the clerk her two tens. While handing her a silver key and a yellow piece of paper from under the carbon, under the receipt page, he said, "Here's your receipt, ma'am. Move in any time."

Ruby took the key, slipped it into one of the pockets of the jean jacket she was wearing and turned towards the door of the hotel, to go and get her bundle of stuff that she'd stashed in another part of town.

The night air felt good to the woman as she quickly walked along the sidewalk, passing the Dixieland jazz club next door to the Harbor Hotel. The mist from the bay lingered in the air as the roar of the cars racing over the freeway above added a rumbling tone to the music of the City. As the texture of night mixed with street lamps and neon light, surrounding sounds of fire sirens, ambulance cries and police car screams mingled with tones of invisible street musicians and jukebox melodies.

Listening to this chaotic symphony, Ruby buttoned her jacket. Then she shoved her hands into her pockets and hurried towards the park, hoping that Jules, the craftsman that she'd left her canvas and her dog with, would still be there. In the distance, she could see that the square where she'd left him was now empty.

"Oh, hell!" she said. "He's gone, and taken my dog with him. Now I'll have to wait until tomorrow to paint. I wonder if my other stuff is still on the roof over behind the Beach. Only way to find out is by going there, but I don't wanta walk. I'll have to take a cab or a bus." After this conversation with the air, the woman turned into the wind and walked hurriedly along Market Street until she came to Kearney, having decided that it was easier to walk than try to find something to ride in at the moment.

Strolling by the office buildings in the financial district of Kearney Street into lower Chinatown was a journey past colorful bookstores, liquor stores, bars, old hotels, sidewalks and, occasionally, other people. Some of the passersby wore suits and ties, the travelers coming from or going to bars before they caught the train or the plane or the car. The street people Ruby saw were dressed for the weather, as she was. They were mostly in jeans, sweatshirts, tennis shoes, anonymous clothes that easily blended into the shadows of the skyscrapers, the alleys and the alcoves, in between the spaces of the neon lights.

She went quickly up Kearney Street, past the Chinese park where the elders did Tai Chi every morning, to where the big new TransAmerica Building rose as a needle to the sky. She had finally reached North Beach. Tall, skinny boys with long, stringy hair hung out on the street corners, smoking cigarettes, looking for scores that were never there. "Hey, you got a light?", "You got a cigarette?", "Got any change?". These wre the phrases they called out at the woman hurrying along the sidewalk with her hands stuffed into the pockets of her jean jacket and her cap planted firmly on her head.

Such a visage turned her into another anonymous, sexless, ageless figure, just a piece of motion, moving through the streets of the city with a destination. She had no time to stop and pass out lights or change and cigarettes. Ruby was trying to get her life together at last, after all these past months of living outside, crashing in doorways or on rooftops, washing in gas stations and restaurants, with no definite place to stay, other than the park or the backseat of an old car down by the pier at the end of the Embarcadero. Sometimes she'd stayed up all night in a 24-hour restaurant, or ridden the bus out into the country, just to hitch-hike back again to the streets of the city.

After all of this hell, all of the misery of poverty and lost identity, Ruby decided to try and stop living like a refugee in her own country. But this had only come about because someone had decided to give her a chance to live inside again and make a home for herself. She needed a safe place to stay. A place like the room she had just rented in the Harbor Hotel. She wouldn't have to be afraid of being rousted or busted for vagrancy or lack of proper ID there. The woman didn't know why her luck had suddenly changed, but she was thankful for this chance to live inside again, like people did, like she had when she'd lived with her family when she'd been a child, before the hospital and the acid trips.

'Wow, what a journey, a nineteen-year-long vacation. Who does that?', she thought as she started to remember scenes from her previous life. She remembered her parents and wondered how they were doing. 'Whatever happened to the Smiths, and the others I used to know? Whatever happened to Reaper? I wonder if he still goes to work at the jailhouse every day. Wow, what a number he was ... I'll never live with anybody like him again.'

Ruby had first met Reaper years before in a folk music club on Upper Grant Avenue in San Francisco. He was playing there, and one evening after his set a mutual friend had introduced them to each other. They'd smiled and nodded, had a cigarette and a drink together, and then didn't see each other again for a decade. Ten years later, that same mutual friend had bumped into Ruby on the street and told her that Reaper had been seen panhandling and playing on street corners for change. Ruby had run into him a few nights later, on the sidewalk down from the music store. He was broke, and playing laments on a sad guitar.

Seeing her approach, he'd said, "Hi, how are you? Long time no see! Could you loan me $10.00? I'm working the streets and will pay you back eventually."

Ruby, who had just gotten her annual birthday check from her father, was flush and said, "Sure!", thinking that she didn't care if he paid her back or not.

Reaper had said, "Gee, that's nice of you. You got

a place to stay also?"

"Yeah, I got a room in the Beach, what about you?"

"I'm staying with some friends from the East Coast. We can go over there if you want to. I've played about eight hours, made enough to contribute to the rent but not much else. That's why I had to borrow the $10.00 from you."

"Oh, that's okay." Ruby'd said, "No big deal. Forget about it, pay me back anytime."

"Okay, I'll do that. You wanta take a bus ride up to the Haight with me? Maybe we can score some acid and a couple of jays along the way."

The two had caught a green city bus and rumbled away along Market Street, up to the Haight. They got off there and after a short walk entered an apartment full of people. Another acquaintance of Ruby's, whom she'd met briefly a few years before, was playing a soft folk guitar at the kitchen table, mumbling the words to her song. Ruby and Reaper nodded and had gone into the living room. There was a joint going round, passing through the hands of the other people there. Exchanging smiles and glances, they'd nodded and sat down.

After a few tokes, Ruby had decided to split for the streets to get a pizza and a bus back to the other side of town. "Thanks for the smoke man, I'll catch you later ... ", she'd said to Reaper.

"Yeah, sure ... thanks for the bread. See you around." Feeling good and slightly high from the jay, and the sight of people playing and being happy, Ruby had passed quickly along the Haight-Ashbury streets that night. She'd remembered the acid she'd left at her pad, and was starting to look forward to her next trip.

Someone else's words started running through her head: 'Been down so long, it looks like up to me ... ' she thought. 'Been off acid so long, life's just another trip to me. I just hope this tab's better than the blotter. That had so much speed in it, real Mickey Mouse stuff. Everybody threw up as soon as they took it. Wow! I wonder whatever happened to Owsley's formula, or if there's any White Lightning left. Rainbow was pretty good for awhile, until they started cutting it with coke and heroin. Why would anyone cut LSD with heroin? Probably all they had, ran out of lactose and powdered milk ... '

Such were the thoughts running through Ruby's head as she hurried through that night, past the buildings and the other people of the evening. Just another soul lost in the moonlight of underworld delights, eagerly running towards oblivion, tired from too much sunlight.

Now, many years later, Ruby again raced through the twilight, chasing thoughts of her old acid days away, hoping that her pillowcases of stuff were still on the roof. She'd left them there that afternoon, on the other side of North Beach, while she'd gone to look for a room. She entered the nightclub section where Finocchio's sign blinked the name of the clown, while down the street the gangster mannequin of bootleg fame rose above the desolate kingdom of strip joints, girlie shows, live sex acts, restaurants, bars and banks. Ruby looked up at the statue of Big Al, as she had so many times before for so many years. She always wondered if that was how Al Capone had really looked.

Crossing the street at Broadway, remembering the song about the guy who could play the guitar, and who wouldn't leave till he was a star on Broadway, she quickened her step. She ran up Upper Grant Avenue, past the old Dante Hotel, the bars, past the hill leading to Coit Tower, along the residential streets until she finally stood panting in front of the yellow-painted wood building with the stone steps. It was on the roof of this apartment house that Ruby has stashed her stuff.

She'd slept on this roof for the past few nights because the fellow who had the apartment at the top of the stairs was an old friend of hers from the San Francisco Art Institute, where she'd studied filmmaking for a few years. Punk would let Ruby go through his refrigerator and take showers there, just because he was a nice guy. He even let her sleep on the floor of his room for awhile, until Ruby decided to move to the roof. She didn't want to have an affair with Punk; she just wanted him to share what he could with her, like a brother would. To a degree he was content with the relationship, but was disappointed that Ruby was apparently incapable of any real affection for him. Occasionally she allowed him to hug her, and she would hug him back, but always pulled away if he attempted to start anything that she considered "funny stuff" or "fooling around".

Something had happened to Ruby shortly after she'd come to San Francisco from that other state. She'd had a baby, and someone had killed it. She had never gotten over this. The nervous breakdown that resulted seemed to be permanent. The disability income that she got in the form of a check every month kept her out of the hospital. For years she was able to exist on this minimal amount of money, dividing it among clothes, movies, candy, drinks and occasional meals.

Ruby'd been living in a hazy dream all her life, with shock after shock bombarding her from the outside. She remembered her mother beating her, and how her father had slammed her face into the keyboard of the piano because she'd been repeatedly playing a passge incorrectly. After that, she'd felt alienated from her parents and had identified with a girl she'd read about in the newspaper, a girl of thirteen, her own age, who had slashed her wrists. When Ruby's mother found her in the bathroom one evening with blood running down her hands from the razor wounds on both her wrists, she knew that something was seriously wrong with her daughter. Shortly thereafter, Ruby's parents drove her to the state mental hospital and left her there.

Her father gave her a tape of Requiem Canticales, a profane piece of classical music, with songs in choral arrangements. Ruby was given a room by herself for awhile. She would listen to the tape over and over again, while thinking of her parents and looking at the bandages that were gradually replaced by thick scars criss-crossing her wrists.

After six months, she was allowed to mingle with the other patients in the day room. At first Ruby missed her solitude, but eventually she became curious about these other women and girls who'd been locked away by their families. Some of the people had been there for 10 or 12 years. Who knew what they thought about, or if they were even able to think any longer?

The doctors there liked Ruby because she had a pretty face. They wanted to make this child want to live rather than die, so they'd treated her with LSD and Stelazine, gradually increasing the dosages at intervals over several months. Meanwhile, Ruby had begun to plot with two other girls as to how they might escape the hell their parents had placed them in.

One night it happened. For some reason all three of them were to be escorted through the tunnels underneath the hospital for disciplinary purposes. For what was unknown. The treatment took place in an area known to the other patients as "The Dungeon". The one guard who was taking the girls to the punishment room never expected such a thing as an escape to happen, but it did. The woman was overpowered, her keys were taken ... the keys to the doors to the outside! Ruby had to choke her, and then the three of them ran, fumbling with the keys to undo the locks to the doors that partitioned the long, winding labyrinthian underground from the outside. Finally, after what seemed like hours, the break was made.

Remembering that time as she climbed the outside staircase to the roof to get her pillowcases made Ruby remember that this was another break. She was escaping from Punk's refrigerator, shower and roof. She was escaping from the psychological trap he'd been able to get her in because her dope bills had become larger than her monthly check. She was escaping from the pain he'd put her through by telepathically demanding the kind of response from her that she was not able to give.

As she climbed past Punk's apartment she looked

in the window. The light in the kitchen was on but the room was empty. The curtains were drawn across the bedroom windows, where another light was on. She could hear music coming from the radio or stereo. 'He's having a good time with himself as usual', Ruby thought, 'well, good for him! I'm gonna get my stuff and take it to my place, and get my own TV and stereo and radio, and have myself a good time too! Just me and Ivy, we're on our own and won't have to be dependent on any guy for a place to stay and something to eat. Yeah, we're gonna be okay.'

Those were Ruby's thoughts as she stepped onto the roof and saw that her pillow-cases were still there, in the corner across from the TV antenna where she'd left them earlier. "Thank God!" she exclaimed, then looked up at the sky as two far distant bright lights darted by. "I wonder if they're UFOs. Sometimes think they might be. Oh, well ... ", she said with a shrug of her shoulders. "That's none of my business. I gotta get my stuff back to the Harbor, then tomorrow get Ivy and a few other things. Yeah, we're gonna have a home at last. No more baths in the gas station bathroom or having to sit up all night in the 24-hour restaurants."

Gingerly grabbing each stuffed pillowcase and tying the ends together with string, Ruby made a handle with which she could carry the bundle down the staircase, past the windows of Punk's apartment, through the streets of North Beach, only occasionally having to stop for a rest. After a couple of hours the familiar freeway was in sight, with its sounds of the cars roaring through the night. The fire sirens screamed in the distance and ambulances rattled by, going on to their various destinations.

The Dixieland jazz notes from the band that played in the club next to the Harbor stumbled through the air as people in tuxedos and sequined gowns stood outside listening to the sounds of the underground. The riffs of the cornet, bass, electric guitar, jazz violin and drums floated into the night-filled atmosphere. The people in evening clothes hardly noticed the ragamuffin staggering by the two pillowcases and exhausted eyes. Those who did registered expressions of distaste, dismay, indifference and distrust. After all, it wasn't their affair about how some people chose to spend their lives, chose to throw their time and away on drugs and madness.

Ruby cared less than nothing what those rich people standing on the sidewalk thought. She had a lot of money in her shoe and more in the bank. She didn't need their sympathy, only their money in the form of tax dollars ... but Ruby never thought about that. She knew her parents had a lot of money. Her father owned condominiums in Florida, and her mother owned her own home in Arizona.

'Yeah, they have a lot of money and places to stay', she thought as tears started to fall from her eyes. She whipped them away with the sleeve of her jacket. 'Now I've got my own place too, yeah. I'll make it real pretty, and pay the rent on time, and everything will be fine.'

In the Harbor, George was looking out the windows of the lobby. When he saw the woman who'd rented the room earlier approaching with the two pillowcases tied together by a piece of string, he gently smiled and opened the door from the inside so the new tenant wouldn't have to break her stride.

"Thanks", Ruby said, darting through the opening.

"Okay, doll. Guess I'll see you later. Going home now? Pretty tired, huh?"

"Yeah." Ruby stopped for a moment to catch her breath.

"That all the stuff you got?" asked George. He looked at the two pillowcases sadly dragging along the linoleum-covered floor behind the ragamuffin in jeans and sweat-shirt as she headed toward the antique elevator.

"No, get the rest of it tomorrow, gotta rest now, goodnight ... "

"Goodnight."

As the old doors of the elevator swung open and Ruby dragged her belongings inside, George lit a cigarette and walked over to the lobby windows, wondering who he'd have to open the door for next. The songs playing on the jukebox next door mingled with the Dixieland tunes of the nightclub on the other side of the old hotel. The sirens of the night added violent orchestration that sounded throughout the waterfront, acting as a background to the sad ballet that the derelict inhabitants in the lobby seemed to dance as they moved back and forth from chairs to the door to the ashtray to the elevator and then to the chairs once more. The gait of these old people swayed to an invisible beat, like a dance of souls who could no longer feel the heat.

Ruby stood inside the old elevator, wondering if it would safely deposit her and her possessions on the third floor. Clang, rattle, the landing was shaky. After much exertion, the metal gate opened and Ruby got her things out into the hallway. She walked down the corridor towards her room, number 314. Fitting the key in the lock, she was happy to see that it worked as the door swung open. She saw that someone had brought her clean sheets, pillows, pillowcases, blankets and towels, all left neatly stacked on the little table next to the floor lamp. The window had been opened to air out the musty room.

As the night chill was increasing, Ruby closed the window, turned on the hotplate for warmth, and looked through the pillowcases for the instant coffee jar and other foodstuffs she'd carefully secreted between newspaper-wrapped dishes, cups and pans. She extracted a pan to boil water in, a ceramic mug wrapped in a tee shirt, some sugar and instant milk powder. Ruby then took out a can of Campbell's black bean soup taken from Punk's kitchen, a bit of cheese wrapped in tinfoil and a few pieces of bread with margarine on them.

'Wow, this'll do fine for supper! I'll heat up some soup, make some toast and have a cup of coffee', she thought. 'Look out the window, listen to the music, keep warm under the covers ... I might even explore the hallway for the shower, and then maybe have a joint. Wow! God's good, He helped me find this neat place where I don't need a radio or a stereo, and have a view like a picture postcard of the San Francisco Bay. Maybe after I get settled and get the rest of my stuff I'll take a ferryboat ride to Marin, get off in

Sausalito, walk around, look in the store windows, maybe go to a restaurant ... '

Looking at herself in the mirror above the dresser, she thought, 'I'll try to fix myself up, maybe get a new jacket, maybe a whole new outfit, go to a professional place to have them trim my hair, get a manicure ... but that costs a lot of money these days. I don't look bad. I'll feel a lot better after dinner and a shower.'

Ruby continued rummaging through the pillowcases looking for a can opener, thinking of how she was going to put the water in the pan, set the pan on the hotplate, make a cup of coffee first, then put the soup on while toasting a piece of bread on the other burner. She'd add a piece of cheese on top to melt as the bread was toasting. The cheese was left over from the chunk she'd gotten at the giveaway line at the mission the other day. There hadn't been enough to go around, so by the time she'd gotten there after Punk had told her about it, they'd started cutting the five-pound blocks in half for the people that were left.

While she was waiting for the water to boil and tasting a piece of the cheese, Ruby thought of her dog Ivy, and wondered if she was having a good time at the street vendor's place. Jules sold leather belts and other things he made in the square in back of the Hyatt Regency. He liked to watch Ivy when Ruby had to go someplace that might not like dogs. She didn't know where he lived, but knew that Ivy'd be all right with Jules.

Finding the can opener, she opened the soup and poured it into the pan, having already made her coffee while she was looking. Doing two things at once was easy for Ruby. Sometimes she'd find herself doing three, four, five things at once. Putting a little bit of water in the pan, she stirred the black contents and turned the heat of the hotplate down while looking for another cup to put the soup in. She found one wrapped in a sock with newspapers around it and inspected it to make sure it was suitable as a container for such hot stuff.

Pouring the soup into the cup was a trip for Ruby. On the elevator up she'd dropped a tab of LSD that was left over from her nights on the roof at Punk's. It was just starting to come on. Her motions started to slow down as her perceptions changed, and the bed started to sway to the music coming in through the window from the jukebox next door. "Wow!" Ruby said, sitting on the floor, trying to look at the soup she was going to have for her supper. Suddenly it seemed too hot, and she wasn't hungry anymore, so she put the cup in the refrigerator for later and turned off the hotplate.

The walls of the room began to be covered with a paisley pattern of purple, blue, green and red colors playing off the texture of the room. "Wow!", she said, "this stuff is too much. Wonder what they cut it with this time? This new Horus blotter acid's right out of the lab, I bet."

Ruby stood up,stretched, got on the bed, looked out the window, then turned around, looked around the room and put herself into a lotus position, trying to concentrate on her mantra. She'd never done this on LSD before.

She found that it was not as easy as it usually was. Acid seemed to disengage her concentration. Even when she shut her eyes the colors and patterns were still there, as though there was a Saturday morning cartoon show going on in her head.

Yes, there was Mickey Mouse and Pluto, but after awhile Ruby found it too tiring to concentrate on the story line of this particular TV show. She first extended one leg in front of her and then the other. She looked at the pillowcases, remembered what she'd been wanting to do for the last couple of days, then got off the bed to pick up the towels, the soap, shampoo and the key.

Glancing around, with the bundle of stuff in her arms, she decided that everything was okay and went out the door, carefully looking from side to side as she went down the hall to the shower. The walls of the hallway rippled, as though swaying to the tunes coming up from the jukebox that could be heard all over the floor.

Reaching the end of the hall, she looked down the next corridor and saw that the plaque on the door nearby said SHOWER in large, vibrating letters. Paisley rainbow patterns were running over the surface of the wood, with cartoon characters dancing through the kalaidescopic tapestry of weaving colors. Forcing herself not to get hung up on these pictures, Ruby turned the knob of the door and opened the wooden panel onto a room of little square tiles and a ledge.

The wide space of a shower stall was in front of her. 'Wow', she thought, 'I could plug up the drain and make a swimming pool ... but better not do that this time. Just try to take a shower.'

Putting down the towel, soap and shampoo and turning on the faucet, she saw that the water danced in colors also; and then, after taking off her jeans, shirt and shoes, she saw that the cartoons and paisley pattern were all over her body, as though she were a tattooed lady. "This is too much ... " she said, while soaping up a lather of the shampoo and the bar of lavender soap that she'd brought with her. "I better not stay here forever, though ... better get through this shower in one piece. Rinse all this stuff off, get dried off and back in the room before anyone knows I'm on acid. Yeah."

And that is what she proceeded to do. Rinsing off, trying to get all the paisley lather out of her hair and off her body, finally doing it. Turning off the water, drying off with the towel, shaking her hair, pulling on her clothes. Carrying her shoes, Ruby stealthily opened the door, then looked up and down the corridor as though everything was fine. She tripped back to number 314, not bumping into anyone in the hallway, and properly fitted the key into the lock.

She opened the door with a jerk, slipped in, tossed the towel on the bed and collapsed into the chair. She turned her head to look out the window at the fire escape and her view of the bay, through which the Embarcadero freeway cut ungraciously. She lay down on the bed, looking at the rush of cars as they race along the concrete bridge a few yards from the fire escape outside the windows of the room. As her eyes closed, a dream of shattering, crumbling, shaking buildings began.

In the dream she was outside on the sidewalk in front of the hotel. There was a 'condemned' sign on the front door in back of her. It was an empty building and everyone was gone. She was there renewing old memories, and because she wasn't in bed in her dream, she walked away.

The acid she'd taken earlier had been especially good. She'd had some things to think over in her mind and LSD always helped her focus on the important aspects of her existence, such as her place in the universe. She noted this as soon as the LSD came on. It usually took about five or ten minutes to get started and it lasted a lifetime. While on LSD, Ruby would do the things she usually did, but every trip was different. This time, in her dream she was on a long walk around the city.

From the front of the hotel, she went to all her favorite landmarks and was comparing them and her perception of them on acid with how she found them when not on LSD. The reality of her material existence was always exaggerated on acid. Then she could see how terrible or wonderful things were, knowing that they would not be the same the next day when she was straight again.

This time, in her dream she looked in the mirror and saw herself as a female form, a girl in the universe. She had no illusions as to what that position entailed. It was the subserviant status of a daughter, a sister, an aunt, a wife, a lover, a mother. She could be a secretary, a teacher, a professional, an artist, a dancer, a writer, a musician; but overshadowing whatever career venture she pursued was the reality of femininity, of femaleness, of second class citizenship. She would never be able to escape this physiological cultural gender trap of her body in this lifetime, because people would always remind her of her place on earth.

Suddenly, the roar of the automobiles intruded on her dream. They sounded like the constant rumble of a freight train. Ruby opened her eyes to the thundering freeway traffic, zooming by outside her window. She looked around at the blue of the sky past the swaying fire escape outside her room. She sat up, reached for the window, opened it and stuck her head outside. The air felt fresh and new, with the scent of ocean spray.

She listened to the foghorns bellowing in the distance. The deep mellow baritone whole notes were comforting to her. They went with the fog that floated in from the bay and crept along the docks, onto the sidewalks, and into her room through the open window. She loved the mysterious grey of the mist as it drifted so silently through the avenues of the city. It was as the cloak of a grand musician, the phantom of the opera, who could never stay. He was always hurrying away to the stage, where his notes were scheduled to play.

Ruby felt exhausted, recalling her life of the past few months. The nights she'd spent on the roof, in the park, in doorways, sleeping on the back seats of old cars, being terrified most of the time. Never having a space of her own had almost driven her mad. She recalled the many times she'd thought of slashing her wrists again, the way she'd done that night in her parents' bathroom so many years ago. Wanting to chase these thoughts of suicide away, she remembered that she must still be racing on the speed-laced acid from the night before. She decided to roll a joint to cool her mind.

Looking around, Ruby remembered that she'd put the stuff in a can in one of the pillowcases. Getting up from the bed to go through them was a trip and a half. There were so many things still happening, on the walls, the floor, the bed, to distract her. Finally she got to the other side of the room and proceeded to find the pot and papers needed to roll her medicine. When the antidote was prepared, Ruby found a match, struck it and put the flame to the end of the joint while inhaling. She tried to hold the smoke down as long as possible.

As she watched herself in the mirror, she was surprised at how red and puffy her face became. She looked to herself like a little piglet, as though she paying the trumpet like Dizzy Gillespie, with both cheeks puffed out. She remembered hearing someone say that it wasn't proper to have puffy cheeks when playing the trumpet. Ruby thought of Piglet, the little friend of Winnie the Pooh, and how they both belonged to Christopher Robin, the custodian of Pooh Corner. Then she meditated on the fact that this was 1984, in San Francisco, California, and she was just a poor woman with a small monthly pension check renting a room in a hotel. It wasn't easy for a woman alone with only a check to recommend her. Everyone wanted references today: where you'd worked, where you'd lived, where you'd gone to school for the last ten or twenty years.

Ruby thought that perhaps it was the fault of the

century, or the country. She didn't understand, nor could she account for the suspicion that permeated the city. It hadn't been that way in the 1960s when everyone she knew was high all the time. Sharing bread, pads, foods, clothes, even dope had been the natural thing to do.

Ruby'd been trying to find a place to stay for so long. She remembered the hours, the miles she'd covered. Walking around crying because she didn't have all the paper pedigree, all the historical ID the landladies had demanded if she was going to be allowed to give them her money. Money wasn't money when it had to be documented, explained, verified and analyzed like that.

She'd picked up her allowance from the P.O. box the other day, after promising Punk that she'd get her own place and stop haunting his roof, shower and kitchen in the early morning, as she'd been doing for the past month on and off. She had grown tired of the doorways, rooftops and parks she'd been sleeping in for the past four years, since she'd split up with her last longterm lover.

Following her train of thought while watching the fading patterns change on the walls and ceiling of the room, Ruby remembered her identity. She was a painter and a filmmaker, besides being one of the many people hanging out in San Francisco in 1984. She'd been living in the City since 1965, when a boyfriend had brought her there from another state. She'd taken acid, speed, pot, hash, mescaline, peyote, opium, cocaine, glue, oxygen ... she'd been strung out on liquor and other intoxicants for years to kill the pain. But all those actions of her past became nothing more than a hazy blur of rapidly fading memory as Ruby realized that, here and now, she was almost middle-aged.

The acid she'd dropped last night seemed to be wearing off. The joint was also almost gone, as the shadows of lavender blue evening began to float into the room. Sounds from the party going on in the nightclub downstairs grew louder as the laughter of the guests mingled with the tinkle of glasses being toasted in the dining room. Ruby crawled out onto the fire escape and sat there smoking, enjoying the evening. After all, she had a ringside seat; she was going to enjoy it in style.

The exaggerations she always experienced when she was flying were shrinking s her perceptions returned to normal. She lay on the fire escape, looking up at the sky, blowing smoke rings at the stars as the cars on the freeway sped by. Ruby thought about the dreams she'd had last night, and also about the fact that now she'd have to wait for at least a week before she tried to trip again. Every time after she tripped, she felt as though she had gone to confession. It was a catharsis, a cleansing. Now she had to wait, and fill her mind back up before she could empty it out again on LSD, the ultimate psychic purge.

Ruby left the fire escape and sat in the armchair, letting her thoughts run wild. 'Did I really walk all over the city today? That dream ... I was so exhausted after those pillowcases -- arranging everything, taking a shower, sleeping in a bed. A real bed, with pillows and sheets! People who always live inside don't realize what it's like to be at the mercy of the night, to have to sleep with a knife and a dog for protection!' Ruby changed her position in the arm-chair. Hugging her knees close to her chest, she suddenly shivered from memories of her life spent on the concrete. She'd had to use the public restroom in the Embarcadero Square as a bathroom. It wasn't safe; there was always the possibility of being surprised unexpectedly. Her mother didn't have any idea of the life she'd lived.

A strange expression came over Ruby's face as memories of her mother and father drifted through her mind. Shuddering, then rising from the chair, she stretched and pulled off the sweatshirt she was wearing, replacing it with a blue turtle-neck and green arm sweater. The turtleneck was the same dark blue as the almost-new jeans she was wearing. They were so deep a blue that they almost looked black, and blended into the shadows of the evening. One thing Ruby had learned while living as a homeless person on the city's streets was that it was safer to be invisible, or as invisible as possible. Therefore she practiced blending into the shadows of the skyscrapers whenever she could.

She then pulled on her heavy dark blue, almost black peacoat and matching knit cap, and made sure her key and other pieces of paper that she used for ID were in her wallet. She had her Social Security card, and her old student ID from the San Francisco Art Institute. She still had a few dollars left from the $10.00 she'd hidden in her shoe before she'd begun to trip.

'Hmm, Ivy will like what I'm going to get her', Ruby

thought. 'That way, I'll be sure she'll remember me and forget Jules. I had to leave her with him. I hope he's still there. Sometimes he stays later than nine. He must be wondering where I am.'

Ruby cautiously slipped out her door, shut it softly and almost crept to the staircase. Tiptoeing down the two flights, she emerged into the lobby, which was almost deserted. George was behind the desk, reading under the light of a solitary lamp, which also illuminated the cavernous spaces of the foyer of this once elegant stage set. The Harbor had seen better days, as had Ruby and George and all the other denizens of this San Francisco night.

Gliding towards the front door, she nodded at George and drifted out into the shadows, which rapidly engulfed her hurrying frame.Quickening the pace of her tennis shoes, she tripped across the avenues past the Embarcadero's famous Ferry Building, past the grassy knolls at the end of Market Street, into the square of fountains and shadows over which loomed the extravagant Hyatt Regency Hotel. She saw that Jules' leatherworks table was still set up, and there was Ivy, who, upon seeing her, went into the swaying dance with which they always greeted each other.

As Ruby ran towards her dog, glad to have found her, she opened her arms and threw them around the big, beautiful hunk of long blue, white and gray fur as it jumped up to greet her. Ivy was a powerful blue shepherd-collie mix, with just a touch of wolf. Ruby never told anyone about the wolf part. She was afraid that if she did, Ivy would suddenly become illegal, as had everything else that she'd ever formed an attachment to in her life.

She'd found Ivy in the pound when she was just a puppy. That was several years ago. Jules had taken her there so she could find a pet to protect her in her hazardous lifestyle. She'd looked at all of the stray, abandoned, lost and runaway dogs and puppies yelping behind the bars and wire screens of the desolate wasteland of the San Francisco Pound. On her last trip up and down this room with the animal cages on either side, Ruby decided that this time she'd really look. She had to concentrate on this one. After all, it would be a pet that could protect her also. Her girl friend Pat had just run out on her. Actually, they'd had a fight. Pat had broken her nose after Ruby had threatened to slash her wrists again and tell people that Pat had made her do it, or that Pat had done it.

Before Ruby could decide which story she wanted to use, she didn't have a chance to think about it any more. A fist had suddenly slammed into her nose, as the voice of her lover had said in a furious tone, "You wanta see blood? Here! You don't have to slash your wrists, honey!" When Ruby looked, she'd seen a red stream of blood flowing freely from her nose to the floor. Tears had welled up in her eyes and she'd felt a terrible pain begin to pound in her head as she staggered to the edge of the bed and sat down. Then Pat had started in again, saying, "How do you like the color of that blood? Is it good enough for you, even though it came from your nose instead of your wrists?"

As she hugged Ivy, Ruby remembered that horrible incident, and looked around for Jules, to thank him for the dog-sitting job. She had promised him a tab of the new trip that she'd been trying out. Not seeing him anywhere, she decided to write him a note, to tell him that she'd come for Ivy and would try to stop by in a day or two. She found a piece of paper blowing along the flagstone court-yard and used a pencil that was lying on Jules' table to write the note. When it was done Ruby fastened it to a nail sticking out of his display. Untying the rope that had secured Ivy to the nearby fountain, she hugged her again, kissed her, and told her that she had a really great new home to take her to, now that she'd been able to find a room that took both dogs and girls with small incomes.

Ivy was still dancing as she and Ruby left the square for a walk up Market Street. Ruby was taking her to the restaurant that had a special on entrees for $5.00. It was just enough for a girl and a blue shepherd-collie. She could get the steak to go and she and Ivy could have dinner under the stars or back in the room, depending on the weather. Ivy hadn't had a steak in a long time, and Ruby didn't want any more than the salad and roll, with the baked potato on the side.

Ruby was already thinking about the next acid trip and what she'd use it for. She'd had her first acid in the State mental hospital in Michigan. The doctors had given it to her as a last resort, hoping to turn her from being suicidal into normal. Then they'd changed the medication to Stelazine, and, as was usual, had overamped the dosage or given her a trial run on an amount of medication that was too much for her system. Ruby had felt like tearing her skin off that day. She'd told the nurses and had begged them not to give her any more of it, because it was driving her out of her mind. She wasn't able to stay in one place for any period of time. She wasn't able to either it down or stand up, but had to keep on switching between both positions constantly.

The nurses had just laughed at her, as though they didn't believe her. They thought that she was just another patient trying to get out of taking her meds. It was during the overdosing of the Stelazine that she'd strangled the matron and escaped.

She didn't want to go to the Community Mental Health Unit for meds, as the Feds had suggested when they were reviewing her SSI files, because she knew that they'd prescribe the same thing. They always prescribed it. Then Pat had showed up at the bar, and had pursued her, and had also tried to get her to take those horrible round blue tablets for psychosis. Not even Pat had believed her when she told her about the torturous reaction she'd had to this medication that the doctors had prescribed. But that was in the past, and this was another life.

Finally Ivy and Ruby got to the hotel. Ruby had the doggie bag from the restaurant to share with Ivy, and a soda and pack of cigarettes for herself. She couldn't wait to show Ivy their new home.

FINIS

****

Author's Postlude"

****

The sound of the rain is as a melody of fragility interspersed with the grey cat's meows, begging for pets as he lingers beside me, rubbing his head against my hand as it holds the notebook. There is a peaceful gentleness here. I give him a hurried caress as he takes his paw away from my foot. The falling drops add a metallic dimension and I yell "Ow!" as the grey cat's claws dig into my bent thigh before he wanders off to lick himself in the rain.

Our maple trees provide a mild leaf cover, which resembles a ceiling of green blocking the sky when I look up. Thick ivy vines shoot from the sides of the house, which is covered in leaves, as are the red-bricked sides of college buildings.

I hear a gentle patter above as the dogs wander from the living room into the bedroom. We are hidden away here, in our blue bungalow, away from the traffic and parades, away from the wandering tourists. I go back into the kitchen to continue ironing the costumes for tomorrow. The radio plays a tune by Count Basie, "You Give Good Love".

I remember the cover of the book, "I Am A Lover", author unknown, a book of U.S. Camera type photographs that came out in the 1950s. On the cover is a picture of a warehouse nightclub with a big parking lot, and a backdrop of the rising hill in the background that held the wooden steps going up to Coit Tower. Allen Ginsberg's "Sun Flower Sutra" talks about these wooden stairs and how one Sunday morning he and Jack Kerouac went down them to the San Francisco Embarcadero, to sit on a stoop and think about the graveyard of San Francisco cablecars. There's also a picture of Bob

Kaufman as a young poet in the Coffee Gallery on Upper Grant Avenue in North Beach during the 1950s in this book.

Meanwhile the jazz on the station playing now is called "Today's Jazz", as the radio DJ comes on to remind us of what we're listening to. The rain has stopped for awhile. We sorely needed it. I planted four acorns the other day ... maybe in a few years we'll have four new oak trees in the back yard. It's a standard city lot.

Our kitchen is like a sauna today; as I iron the pants' pastel stripes, sweat falls into my eyes. I light a Gauloise, take a sip of wine, listen to the tune "Walking To Freedom" on the jazz station while writing another sentence. This is how books are made, a sentence at a time. The phone rings; a pre-recorded message comes on, then I ask if there's anybody there. It is a silent line. I hang up and pour another glass of California wine.

I call my mother. She's home in Chico, California, working in a movie called "Sleeping Dogs Lie", playing a character similar to herself, and has three pages of dialogue. I tell her about my supervisor. She says to pray for him. I say I'll offer up a novena for him. She tells me not to smoke, not to drink. I agree with her. She reads me her poetry over the phone. I agree with her. Eventually she says I'll run up the phone bill. We say goodbye.

Gail's going to visit her mother tomorrow with a load of presents for her 85th birthday. I told mine I'd be sending her $100.00 this September. Meanwhile I light a cigarette, take a sip of wine, start the washing machine. There are chores to be done around the house when I get home: laundry, trash, all the things a housekeeper would do if we had one.

I can retire in seven years. Mother says this is the life I have chosen for myself. I agree and bemoan the plight of the street people on the streets of San Francisco. She tells me there are a thousand people living in the park, Golden Gate Park. I think they should all be put up at the Presidio.

"Rooftops", one of the plays in Street Kids and Other Plays published in 1995, is about a group of people living in a park in San Francisco in 1980. Eventually this place, called Wino Park, was shut down by the City. It was too popular. People were afraid to go into it, as the characters inhabiting it gave the appearance of being drunk, high, stoned and disorderly. Also the city had provided giant tubes to be used as sleeping quarters, and naturally these units became places of business. Whatever underworld dealings there were to conduct were conducted in the tubes.

I remember guys that used to stand on the corner selling valium and librium. They were selling their prescription medication for fifty cents to $2.00 a pill and then using the money to live on, in whatever fashion they chose: Small Business Enterprise. I used to watch them, when I had time, from the windows of our room in the hotel across the street. The show was especially good at three or four in the morning, after the bars had closed. It was an on-going after hours club. They have such clubs on the East Coast too, but these are held in people's basements or apartments much of the year. The weather in California is a year-round paradise for such small business activities.

But on this particular Sunday in Albany, New York I'm excited about completion of my application to the College of St. Rose for a Master's in English. The psychology program at Russell Sage proved in the end to be disheartening. The professors there disapproved of my point of view as much as I disapproved of theirs. And even when I wrote the truth about people and situations that were a part of my background, the teachers believed the details were fiction, and that my view of their discipline was less than serious. This problem shouldn't come up in the English program at St. Rose.

So meanwhile, fifty years down the road from the start of this story, my brothers and sisters grew up; some got married. My mother has ten grandchildren and one great-grandchild. Tony lives in Sonoma County, California. He tells people that he's the real Anthony Burgess and has written a shelf of books to prove it. Andrew is dead. It could have been murder; it could have been suicide. He died in Reno, Nevada after getting back from his brother-in-law Craig's funeral.

Philip is haunting my mother in Chico; he's trying to shock her to death from what I hear. He builds ships and fixes cars and trucks; perhaps he'll decide to build his own house one day. Jimmy is a cowboy with a gang of guys in Half Moon Bay. Last I heard he was doing okay. He's fifty-one now, another senior citizen. Christopher has diabetes; they're treating his insulin blindness with lasers. Peter is a member of the National Guard now. He got thrown out of the

Marine Corps for fighting with another officer. Mari-Beth, Craig's wife and now his widow, has three daughters: Starla, Jaydee and Amber. They're studying to be a doctor, a lawyer and the other, who's just had a baby herself, undecided. Sylvia is the youngest, but she's about thirty now. She has a few children, and likes to drive Mercedes Benz cars and go scuba driving.

Kathy shot herself in the head with a rifle one night in 1974. Her husband ran out the door, jumped into his truck and drove away. He was running from the bullets flying through the air; he'd taught her how to shoot deer. Veronica used to look like me when we were children, and was heartbroken when I ran away. Since then we've only written a few times. She's married with a couple of kids, living in California. My father died in Chico, at Mari-Beth's house in 2001. He'd lived by himself in San Francisco, counting the years on his car as if it were a baby he was raising.

My mother was involved in the adventure of a small part in the movie "Sleeping Dogs Lie". Recently, when I heard that she was in a movie being filmed in Chico, I asked her to write her impressions of the experience. She graciously sent me back the following words:

Mary Jane: I refuse to settle into old age gracefully, and intend to continue to look for new avenues on which to ride and expand my views. That experience as a part of the cast of "Sleeping Dogs Lie" by Chris Sutton of Oberon Productions taught me that I'm not yet ready to just quietly disappear as women of my advanced age are supposed to do. The different phases that we all went through reading for the part and the resultant applause evidently was something I really needed to bolster my spirit, and showed me that I still have the notion that I am somebody, although many of the members of my immediate family would decry such an attitude.

We endured weeks of rehearsals without scripts for this movie. In motion picture making, small segments of the whole are shot, and the final film is put together by technicians in the editorial room. The whole experience was quite a revelation to me, for I had never realized before the extent of the technical aspects of the motion picture.

We had one actual full reading with the majority of the cast present when the author/director Chris Sutton clued the newcomers such as myself to the scene as to the technical aspects of how a movie is made. We met one another and then dispersed. About a week later I was called on the phone to come at 2:00 a.m. in the middle of the night for my scene. WOW! The idea of riding my bike along the darkened streets of Chico to say my lines before a Panavision movie camera really caused me to have "What am I about to do?" feelings! However, I did it. I rode my bike to the small house that was the set and waited and waited and waited.

Then I was told I would be called to return a few days later. This time the more reasonable hour of 4:00 p.m. was set, and I arrived a half hour earlier. Make-up was applied and the dress I was to wear was given to me by the wardrobe mistress, Maria Rivera, and I changed in the motor home belonging to the head cameraman. Then I was ushered into the room of the small house, shown the rocking chair I was to sit in, and met the actor who had driven up from Sacramento where he was appearing in a play. He was an intense young man: something about him reminded me of the impression I'd received of Jack Lemmon when I was hired as an extra in the movie "The Days of Wine and Roses", in which he and Lee Remick starred.

The actor suggested we go over our lines together, and when we came to the line, "Sharp as a tack and twice as ornery", he suggested that I change it to "ornery as a mule" because "a tack is hardly ornery". Well, when I thought about all of the tacks and nails I've tried to nail during my 76 years I must say that tacks can be quite ornery. So during the several takes that were made, half the time I followed his suggestion and half the time the script. It was a most intense experience, for it was a small space occupied by the guy holding the microphone, the author/director, the director, the cameraman, his assistant, the wardrobe mistress, and the many other artists, plus the two of us upon whom all attention was focused.

The camera was in back of the rocking chair I was seated on, due to necessity to capture the facial expressions of the actor as he spoke his lines. Then after several takes, the camera was moved to the corner off my left, and there I was with the $350,000.00 Panavision camera pointed at me. The cameraman, his assistant and all others in the room now came to attention. The director measured the eye level from my eyes to the door for some peculiar reason, then said we would do some practise run-throughs. We did.

Evidently they were acceptable and the words, "This is a take" sounded as a square numbered object was held in front of me and then drawn away, and after several run-throughs I heard the words, "This is a wrap" and that was that. I was on film and eventually on my way to Europe where grade B movies from America are first distributed after appearing at the Stardust Film Festival somewhere. It was a truly memorable experience. I enjoyed the friendliness of the young people while we awaited our call at the motor home. I may have been assigned the role of the elderly woman Reba, but I didn't feel old and I refuse the mantle of the elderly no matter how many times it is draped upon me.

I have never learned how to make the most of the talents I was blessed with at birth, and have only stumbled and struggled through life with few friends and many enemies for whatever reasons. Even so, little Mary Jane Green Sconberg Burgess has finally grown up and found her place on the screen of time. The first part I had in a play was as the witch in "Hansel and Gretal" in which I managed to completely wreck the carefully constructed house in the third act on the stage of the George Peabody School in San Francisco, or was it the Alamo? And here again, when I'm seventy-six I'm called upon to play the role of somebody akin to a witch! I have enjoyed acting more than I ever let myself really believe.

It was great to be able to finally talk plain after having been, among other things, the victim of stuttering during my childhood years, and I'm glad that once again I trod the boards in the movie, "Sleeping Dogs Lie".

Brio: And with these words from my mother, to whom

this book is dedicated, I will close my own account of these adventures. For those who survived them, I wish good things in the times ahead; for those who have gone beyond, I wish their souls peace and rest.

And for the many of you who read of the adventures of those -- living and dead -- who participated in the events depicted herein, I wish at least a modicum of understanding and compassion for those whom you met in this book, and any similar others whom you may chance to meet in person during your own lifetimes.

The End

ABOUT THE AUTHOR

Currently living in a dream … William Burroughs was sitting next to me, there was a note from him on the piano; we were talking … I was talking … it was in a cabin, outside were people doing and scoring … as on a busy urban sidewalk, or a street in North Beach …

He suddenly got up and ran out … I woke up, thought about it, wondered if he'd left because I talked too much … he'd been married and used to talk to his wife, and then she'd talk to him … I think I'd been playing the piano … after the storm. A lightning show with thunder for cymbals crackled while rumbling through the sky. God's the best artist of us all … I've another book of dreams waiting to be written …

Now that I've retired from my day job, I've been employing my degrees at night … that's when I write … when it's darkly bright with misty moonlight …

War is Death
Memorial for James C. Burgess

Timor mortis conturbat me

Veteran WWII
The African/Italian Front of
the European Theater
1942-1945

There is no time for closure when the
bullet hits the bone
and the skull shatters as though
bludgeoned by a stone ...
death in war ...

no time for funerals or memorial services ... just
keep on going, dodging the pellets exploding
all around you ...
zig zag up the sand into the thick of the action ...

reach the bunkers, keep firing and shifting, outsmarting
the bullets flying, with the bombs
falling from the sky, keep on running, firing
seeking shelter while trying to cover
buddies caught in the thick of the action ...
death in war ...

it's not polite, it's not gentle with
fond memories being passed around,
just grab the dog tags and move on
to the next body, higher ground ...

grab the dog tags, help with the body

bags ... pick up the arms and legs, pick up
the heads, hands and fingers, pick up the
noses that have been blown off ...
death in war ...

there's no time for sadness
just keep on moving, keep on
carrying the pack that's got the
first aid kit, the c rations,
the grenades hanging from your belt,
the bullets in your pack ...

don't let them get wet, that's all that's
saving you from death ... from the body bag ...
fox holes, holes in the ground dug with
a short spade that's in your pack, fox
holes on a beach head ... bullets flying

through the air, blood, bones, torn
flesh
everywhere ... no cigarette breaks, no
coffee breaks, no dinner, breakfast,
lunch or nap breaks ...
death in war ...

war is death ... War is Death.
... war is hell, war is chaos
that four years would take 60 years to forget
and then only death brings closure because
there is no forgetting ...

PRAISE FOR WORKS BY BRIO BURGESS

About *Street Kids, and Other Plays* (Jacob's Ladder Books, 1993)

"This realistic collection of plays chronicles the lives of young people with all the poetry of Shakespeare and the drugs of Sid and Nancy. These street kids are not just about drugs and violence; they have intense feelings, which they express through their poetic speech as well as through song. We see their lives, their loves, and their demons all set to music."

—Kenya McCullum, Hudson Valley Writer's Guild, News Letter Review

About *Saratoga Ice Poems & A Rocking Horse Blues* (Butcher Shop Press, 2000)

"Your poems have ecstasy!"

Saratoga Ice Poems & A Rocking Horse Blues
by Brio Burgess

Your poems
have ecstasy
"in the land of
mind's dream"

— lawrence F

for more information or
to order Butcher Shop Books
send a check or money order to:
Butcher Shop Press
30 West st Apt. 1B
Oneonta, Ny 13820
607-436-8591
butchershoppress@hotmail.com

Cover Photo of Brio Burgess by Jean Wada 1980

www.ingramcontent.com/pod-product-compliance
Lightning Source LLC
Chambersburg PA
CBHW030343310726
48979CB00001B/161

* 9 7 8 1 8 7 7 8 8 0 1 2 4 *